YOUNG GUN

Johnny stood glaring at Maggard, waiting. Maggard stared, not believing that the boy hadn't run off in fear.

Paddy came up behind him, "Johnny, you best back away from this one. He means to kill you." Johnny said nothing.

"Well, kid," Maggard said, "if that's the way you want it, I guess I don't have much choice."

Maggard, sure of himself, swung his pistol to bear on Johnny. In those few seconds, many of those there felt it took an eternity for Maggard to aim and cock his pistol. And in that eternity lurked the pale face of death, and every man in the room felt it.

But in that frozen second, Johnny's hand flew to his pistol, and his hand was a blur of speed that left many a witness dumbfounded to the end of his days. And as Maggard was pulling on his own trigger, Johnny fired, and the room exploded with death. . . .

SUNSET RIDER

Jory Sherman

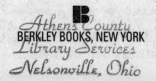

BERKLEY BOOKS, NEW YORK

SUNSET RIDER

A Berkley Book / published by arrangement with
the author

PRINTING HISTORY
Berkley edition / May 2002

Copyright © 2002 by Jory Sherman.
Cover art by Bruce Emmett.

All rights reserved.
This book, or parts thereof, may not be reproduced in
any form without permission.
For information address: The Berkley Publishing Group,
a division of Penguin Putnam Inc.,
375 Hudson Street, New York, New York 10014.

Visit our website at
www.penguinputnam.com

ISBN: 0-425-18552-4

BERKLEY®
Berkley Books are published by The Berkley Publishing Group,
a division of Penguin Putnam Inc.,
375 Hudson Street, New York, New York 10014.
BERKLEY and the "B" design
are trademarks belonging to Penguin Putnam Inc.

PRINTED IN THE UNITED STATES OF AMERICA

10 9 8 7 6 5 4 3 2 1

For Les Williams

Prologue

HE WAS A STRANGE MAN, SOME SAID; A DRIFTER, A loner, a man born for the rope or the bullet. He was also a man bent on vengeance, so blinded by his hatred for one man that he was bound to get into trouble sooner or later.

"But there was strong blood in him," Paddy Osteen, his friend, said, "that made him want to change his destiny."

"Destiny is one thing," Johnny said, for he was a reader of books, "and fate is another. You can't change your destiny, but you can sure as hell change your fate, if you've got the will and the guts."

Johnny Stagg's fate might have been sealed that night when he saw his father murdered, but he would never see it that way. For fate, he would learn, was a twisting, serpentine path through a wilderness teeming with dangerous trails and dangerous creatures, man and beast.

"Sometimes," Paddy said later, "what a man does in one single moment of his early life stays with him the rest of his days. It marks him, like Cain, and from then on, every last day is numbered and counted. I figured to bury Johnny right next to his father not long after he left town."

There were others in the town who felt the same way.

They figured Johnny had just picked the wrong man to kill, and should have kept his pistol in its holster.

"One of these days," his friend Phill Hardesty said, "I'm going to look out the window and see that blue roan of Johnny's come walking back into town with an empty saddle."

"That's probably going to be his fate," Mrs. Lucille Coombs, another of Johnny's friends, said. "He'll get murdered just like poor old Bill."

But Johnny didn't believe a man had to accept either fate or destiny. Like some ancient warrior, he was prepared to battle the gods themselves, if necessary, to avenge the death of his father and change not only his fate, but his destiny as well.

However, the young have no fear of death, and sometimes it comes right out of nowhere and provides both fate and destiny in a single timeless moment.

The trails west are littered with the graves of those who tempted fate and could not change their inevitable destiny.

It was a dark night on the Missouri River, in the Year of Our Lord 1834, when Johnny Stagg embarked on his journey west, knowing he would be both the hunter and the hunted and, like the hero Ulysses, might never return to his home, might never return to Ithaca.

1

EVERY MORNING HE LISTENED TO THE SONGS OF DEATH.
The songs were trilled on the tongues of the women inside the lodges along the river. There was much crying and wailing, too, and those sounds were part of the death songs as well.

He listened to them every morning before the sun arose and spread stains of colored paint on the dark iron of the river. He listened to the songs, and felt the bristles on his neck stiffen and vibrate as if they were tuning forks.

The Osage always remembered their dead before the sun came up each day. They remembered those who were killed in battle, those who died in their sleep or from the coughing sickness, or who had slipped away in the winter of their lives. They sang, too, for their dead dogs and their dead horses. They sang and mourned for all their dead, and he thought it was an odd thing to do. It was, he thought, as if all those people and animals had died in the dark of the night, as if they died every night of their lives and would never stop dying even though they were already dead.

He wondered sometimes if he should not be singing with them, singing for his dead mother. He thought of his mother at those times, and he sometimes sang in his mind or hummed low in his throat so that his father could not hear him in the next room where he lay still sleeping. He did not want his father to hear him, and anyway, he could not make the trilling sounds that the Osage women made with their tongues.

Sometimes, too, he thought of his mother so strongly that he would sob, and that, too, sounded kind of like a song for the dead. He hoped his mother could hear him sob for her, but when he thought about that, he could only see her grave in his mind, could only remember the rough box going into the ground, deep into the earth, and the men shoveling dirt over the box and sealing off his mother forever.

Those were terrible things to think about every morning, and he knew it was probably peculiar of him to listen to the Osage in those hundred lodges remembering all their dead every morning before the sun came up and singing the ancient songs of death so mournful, so sad, it made him cry. And if he did not cry with his eyes, he cried with his heart. Every time. Every day. Every sad, grieving, mother-lonesome morning.

When the keening died down and faded away, young Johnny Stagg crept out of his bunk in the small room next to his father's bedroom and slipped into his boots. He wore his clothes to bed in the summer, even his socks, so he would not have to waste time dressing. His boots were worn and patched, and he was growing out of them as he was growing out of all the clothes his mother had made for him. But he knew how to sew, and his father had taught him how to use the awl to patch leather, and he was good at fixing belts and shoes and moccasins. He had even made a holster for the little .40-caliber pistol his father had given him when he turned eighteen, more than a year ago.

Johnny walked outside through the back door of the

cabin and went to the pump next to the watering trough. He pumped the handle until water began to gush through the spout. He cupped both hands and stuck them under the falling stream of water. He splashed his face, shivering at the coldness, and rubbed his hands over his neck and behind his ears as his mother had taught him to do. The horses in the corral outside the barn whickered, blew steam through rubbery nostrils, pawed the ground.

"All right, all right," Johnny said.

The chanting from the Osage village faded to a murmur, and then shrank to a silence as the boy walked to the barn, opened a door, and went inside. The horses tramped in from the corral and stalked toward him as he filled a pail with oats and corn. One of the horses, his own, a blue roan gelding well over fifteen-and-a-half hands high, rubbed its nose against Johnny's arm, pushing the boy toward the open stall. Johnny poured feed into the bin, and went to the next stall and emptied the bucket as his father's horse entered, its head swaying from side to side, a whinny gurgling in its throat.

"Blue," he said to his horse, "don't you eat all this feed up. You leave some for Molly, hear?

"There you go, boys," Johnny said, slapping the bay mare on the rump as he left the stall. He threw the empty bucket in a corner of the tack room, next to the feed sacks, then closed and latched the door.

Johnny walked out into the dawn, the sky now taking on color in the east, a cream spreading across the distant horizon. The stars had already faded and were no longer visible, and the moon was a pale ghost in the sky.

Out of the shadows of night, he watched the fort emerge on its high hill overlooking the Missouri River, its battlements rising above the high log walls, the barracks tiered above the walls, too, and he remembered the bandy-legged Manuel Lisa walking around its wooden circumference, marking its angles and defenses in a notebook and peering in every nook and cranny inside its walls like a drunken man looking for his shoe.

And he recalled the mountain men who had come through here in buckskins looking like foreign dignitaries from some far-flung land beyond all oceans, and he had stared at Beckwourth's dark skin and wondered if he were a prince from Africa come to hunt lions in the faraway Rocky Mountains.

Once, after the fort was built several years ago, he had seen William Clark talking to the factor, George Sibley, and wished he could have heard what they were saying to each other as they toured the fort that Clark had built with his mind and the force of his personality so long ago. And William P. Hunt had come there, too, on his way to the Rockies, one of the men with a name everyone knew even if they did not know the man himself.

Johnny thought of these things, as he often did, when he first saw the awesome sight of the fort in the morning, and now he walked with purpose to his father's blacksmith shop, there to start the fires for the day's work before returning to awaken his father and tell him the forge was ready and waiting.

He walked with a light step to the shop because he knew work was good for his father, who had brooded and drunk too much since the burying of his wife, Johnny's dear mother, Pauline, a German woman who had never lost her thick Teutonic accent even with her dying breath when she had said, "Ve go now to de vater." Johnny had wondered if she had meant her father or the water, and he had never summoned the courage to ask his father. Her words, like most of her speech, had remained a mystery.

The wind rose off the river as Johnny walked to the shop, his boots crunching on the grit of the road. He waved to the sentry on the wall, but the sentry did not wave back. Johnny sniffed the air and watched the white birds wheel in the wind like flung patches of snow against the blue of the sky. He waved to the gulls, and they waved back and squealed like frightened little girls as the wind wafted them over the river's iron-gray waters.

The shop was cold and dark, but he knew where everything was. The light from the rising sun streamed through the cracks in the back wall in feeble columns filled with dancing dust motes stirred up by his tread. He stacked light dry wood in the forge and picked up a handful of fine shavings for tinder. He stuffed the shavings around the pyramid of kindling wood he had stacked, and then picked up the chunk of flint and the piece of horseshoe-shaped steel he used as a striker.

Snicksnicksnick. Sparks flew into the tinder and clung there like tiny orange stars. Johnny blew on the embers in the shavings and they burst into flame.

He fanned the flames with his hand until the fire was going well, and then started gathering the ironwood and driftwood he had dried and stacked against the side wall. He set the wood down next to the forge, and walked out the back door to watch the morning blossom on the prairie. He saw a pair of swifts dart by, angling through the invisible currents of air like flying fishes.

He turned when he heard a noise inside the shop, knowing who it was who had entered. He turned and walked back inside, irritated that he had to deal with Paddy Osteen and his constant jabber.

"Top o' the mornin' to ye, Johnny-boy." Paddy waddled on bowed legs over to the forge. He held out his hands over the fire and rubbed them as if he was washing them in milk.

"Paddy."

" 'Tis a fine mornin', Johnny-boy."

"I've got to go wake Papa."

"You'd best don a suit of armor then. Your daddy's bound to have a head the size of a pumpkin on him. Stayed late at the tavern, he did, swillin' down the whiskey like a soldier with pay in his pocket, playin' cards until he could no longer see the spots."

"You shut your mouth, Paddy."

"Oh, he's a grievin' man, your daddy is, and he ain't makin' friends at the waterin' hole, no siree."

Johnny frowned and added the hardwood to the fire, moved the coals around with an iron poker. Orange sparks flew up with the flames, and Paddy withdrew his hands. He worried a cud of tobacco in his nearly toothless mouth, tonguing it from one cheek to the other. He scratched the graying stubble on his chin with the vigor of a man ridding himself of fleas.

"You better mind your own business, Paddy."

"Oh, and your daddy's not me business? Who was it gave him comfort when your dear mother died? And who cooked for you both when you was both so stove up with grief you was dyin' of starvation after we buried your sweet darlin' mother?"

"That don't give you no call, Paddy."

"I hate to see a man kill himself with drink that way. Me own brother died of the creature, and me father as well. And my dear father's dyin' killed me mother. Oh, it's a sad thing to see a man go down that drunkard's path, Johnny-boy."

"Papa only drinks because he gets lonesome. It don't get in the way of his work."

"Oh, I'll grant ye, your daddy's not in the grave yet, and it's likely not the likker what will put him there."

"What in hell's name are you talking about, Paddy?"

"Oh, there's talk at the tavern, there is. Your daddy's been winnin' at the cards and there's some what don't like that. Not at all, no, not at all."

"Who's talking?"

"Some."

"Not that Nate Maggard?"

"The very same, boyo. He's a bad one, that Nate."

"Damn," Johnny said, and bent down to put a chunk of ironwood on the blazing fire. He stirred the coals again, showering sparks on Paddy's rumpled and patched duck trousers. Paddy patted the glowing sparks to ashes and danced a little jig as he cracked a toothless smile.

"I guess I'll have to drag Papa away from the table tonight, Paddy."

"Yep, ye will, boyo. 'Specially if he's winnin'. And that won't be easy."

"I got work to do, Paddy."

"Who you got comin' in this mornin', Johnny-boy?"

"Some feller in Sibley. He's bringin' in two mares and a gelding."

"Broke?"

"I sure as hell hope so," Johnny said.

"I'll sweep up." Paddy walked to the back of the shop and found the broom. He started whistling a tune that sounded to Johnny like the melody of an Irish jig.

"What are you so happy about, Paddy?"

"Oh, didn't I tell you? I'm expectin' my dear sister Maureen tomorrow."

"She's coming here? To Sibley?"

"Oh, that she is, Johnny-boy. My dear sister and her lovely daughter, my niece, Caitlin, and Maureen's fine husband, Seamus O'Brien. They're comin' from St. Louis."

"Are they moving out here?"

"Well, now, yes and no. They're passin' through, they are, followin' their dreams like many another who've set foot in this very place."

"Where are they going?" Johnny asked.

"Why, to Santa Fe, the very hub and heart of the West in New Mexico. Seamus is a most enterprisin' young man and he has commissions from several firms in St. Louis to trade for silver and other costly goods. Oh, he'll make money and clothe me sister and me niece in fine silks and expensive baubles."

"I can see why you're excited," Johnny said. "You probably haven't seen your family in some time."

"Aye, that is true, Johnny, me boy. Not since eighteen hundred and thirteen, when I came out here with nothing but my pipe and purse and a tattered Bible."

"I look forward to meeting your sister."

"Oh, it's my lovely niece, Caitlin, who'll catch your eye, Johnny. She's as fair as any colleen you'll ever see, and none sweeter. Just like her dear mother, my sister."

"Just so you don't try to be a matchmaker, Paddy," Johnny joked. "I'm not ready to take on the responsibility of marriage just yet."

"Perish the thought, Johnny-boy, perish the thought. She'll just be passin' through. But who knows, eh? If she catches your fancy . . ."

"Go, on, Paddy. Keep whistling."

Paddy grinned. He began to sweep up the dead little coals round the forge, pushing the pile toward the back. That was Johnny's job, but Paddy always did that when he came to the shop. It made him feel useful, Johnny guessed, and he was grateful for the help.

Johnny walked out front and looked at the river. He could hear the empty bull boats knocking against each other. They made a hollow sound with each lap of wave as the gulls *screed* at a high pitch and flapped overhead like white rags boiled up by the wind that was building over the prairie under the warming sun. He wondered what the Osage were doing now that their grieving was over and the sun was climbing into the sky. He sniffed, hoping to smell what they might be cooking that morning, but the only smells were from the fort, the same old bacon, beans, and biscuits, hard as rocks and filled with weevils.

He lifted the little .40-caliber pistol his father had made

for him. He checked the flint and tightened the screw that held it in place. The pistol wasn't loaded. He might put powder and ball to it tonight when he went to the tavern over in Sibley to watch his father play cards.

His father would hide him good if he ever found out his son was carrying a loaded pistol. Especially into a tavern where rough men were drinking.

Still, it was something Johnny wanted to do. Just in case Nate Maggard tried to do something mean to his father.

Johnny looked down the road. He saw Fred Oldfield walking toward the shop, leading those three horses he wanted shod.

"Paddy, I'm goin' to wake Papa. Here comes Mr. Oldfield."

"Sure, and I'll take care of the gentleman, Seanny. You'll be a while."

Johnny could hear Paddy cackling as he started trotting toward the house, the holster with its empty pistol slapping against his leg. When he had time, he'd have to punch a hole at the bottom and run a leather thong through it so it didn't flop around when he ran.

The cannon at the fort roared, and when Johnny turned around he saw the flag riding up the pole on its lanyard. Just in time to catch the sunshine. It gave him a good feeling to see the flag waving so proudly over Fort Osage.

2

JOHNNY KNEW TO STAND WELL AWAY FROM HIS FATHER'S bed before he awakened him. Waking Bill Stagg could be a terrible experience for anyone within arm's or leg's reach, because Bill Stagg did not like to be awakened from a sound sleep and he always slept soundly—sometimes, Johnny thought, hovering just above the brink of death.

"Papa, you got to get up," Johnny called in a voice soft as a kitten's purr. "You got horses to shoe and the forge is ready. Coffee's ready, too. Papa?"

"Mmmf," Stagg grunted as if he had a piece of pillow stuffed in his mouth.

"Wake up, Papa. Time to get up." A little louder this time. "Smell the coffee, Papa?" The house reeked with the smell of coffee brewed from Arbuckle's roasted beans.

"Gawonk," Stagg said, one arm flailing around for a target. Like a blind man groping for a wall just out of reach.

Johnny edged around the room to the curtained window that faced east. He pulled aside one panel and the sunlight streamed in, washing over Bill's face with paralyzing suddenness. Johnny watched as his father cocked open one eye, then closed it quickly, blinded by the shattering blaze of light.

"Damn you, Johnny," Bill said. "You ought to be horsewhipped."

"Wake up, Papa. Time to go to work."

"I'll be the judge of that."

"Judge not, lest ye be judged," Johnny recited.

"Don't you Bible me, you whippersnapper. And close that damned curtain."

"Soon's you get up, Papa."

Grumbling and growling low in his throat, Bill rolled around on the bed and then slid a leg over the side. Holding an arm up to shield his face, he sat up and swung his other leg over. "I'm up," he said.

"Not all the way."

Johnny began to slide along the wall, away from the window, toward the door and escape. His father finally lunged from the bed and closed the curtain with a violent flourish. Johnny stepped through the door, out of range if his father was going to throw anything at him. He knew his father would not go back to bed. Neither of them ate breakfast since Johnny's mother had died. Neither of them liked to wash breakfast dishes. Cooking and cleaning up just took too much time. But Johnny always looked forward to having coffee with his father. That was when they did their best talking with each other.

"I'll set the cups out, Papa," Johnny called out as he walked to the stove in the kitchen. He knew his father would throw water on his face and put on some overalls and his work boots. Once Bill was up, he stayed up, but it was a powerful chore just to awaken him and get him out of bed. Before he left his father's room, Johnny had seen his father's eyes for just a second. Even slitted as they were, Johnny could tell they were bloodshot. He had heard his father come in the night before, staggering through the front room, crashing into furniture, the wall, and finally falling into his bed. It was something that worried him of late. His father was drinking too much and staying up too late, something his mother would never have allowed while she was alive.

Johnny set two cups on the table and checked the firebox on the little wood-burning iron stove. Enough wood and fire were left to keep the coffee warm. Steam spewed from the spout of the coffeepot, spreading the aroma in vaporous mists all through the house.

Johnny walked to his bunk and picked up the book he was reading. He had fallen asleep the night before while reading it by lamplight and the book had fallen to the floor, but was still open to the page where he had left off when his eyes had drooped shut. The book was one his teacher had given him when he had finished his schooling this past winter. Mr. Mooney said he had gotten it from one of the keelboat men and that it had been all over the world. It was an exciting book, by a Greek named Homer. Mr. Mooney said the book had been translated from Greek into English and that it was a good translation. The book was called *The Odyssey* and was about a man named Ulysses who wandered the seas far from home.

Johnny sat down at the table and began reading. He heard his father thumping around in the next room, but Johnny would not have his coffee until his father came to the table in the kitchen and sat down.

Mr. Mooney had taught Johnny Latin, and he had loved reading about Julius Caesar and his Gallic wars. Mr. Mooney made the translating into a thrilling experience for Johnny.

"Someday, Johnny, I hope you will take up Greek so that you can read the original plays and books in that language. But you've got to give up your wild ways if you would ever be a scholar."

"What's a scholar?" Johnny had asked.

"Someone who cares about ancient literature, as I do."

"I care about the books you give me to read, Mr. Mooney."

"Ah, but you are always fighting and quarreling with your fellows."

"They're the ones who start it, Mr. Mooney."

"I notice that they are the ones with the black eyes, too," Mr. Mooney had said.

"Well, I can't help that."

"You're quick, Johnny, both with your mind and your fists. And one day, the latter will surely get you into a lot of trouble."

"I'll think about being one of those scholar fellows, Mr. Mooney."

And he had thought about it, but he wasn't sure how to go about it now that he was through with schooling. He did like to read and that was one of the things a scholar did, Johnny knew.

"Readin' again, Johnny?"

"Yes, sir. Good morning, Papa."

"Why don't you pour us some coffee, son, and put that book away. You're going to wear your eyes out readin' so much."

Johnny closed the book and set it aside as he got up to pour their coffee into tin cups. His father, once tall to him, but now a few inches shorter, sat down at the table. He was a lean man, like his son, but had more bulk to him than Johnny. He also bore a mustache, which Johnny did not, and handsome sideburns that were like matted black wool. He and Johnny both had straight lean noses and dark brown eyes, hair to match, hair that was thick and curly when it needed cutting. Johnny had his mother's sensual mouth, while Bill's lips were thinner.

"How do you feel, Papa?" Johnny set a cup in front of his father and sidled around the table to sit down with his own steaming cup.

"I feel one hunnert percent, like always."

"You got the red eye, Papa."

"Don't you start on that, Johnny. You sound like your mother, God rest her soul."

"Yes, sir. I don't mean to carp at you like Mama did."

"She didn't carp at me, son. She was just watchful. Maybe a mite too watchful over me at times."

"Well, I reckon Mama was watchful over me, too."

"Oh, you were a caution, son, not only when you was a tyke, but now. I thought I told you to stay away from them docks. That old wider woman, Missus Tabor, come by the shop yesterday to tell me you and her boy, Willis, got into it down there. Nothing but riffraff down on the waterfront I keep tellin' you."

"You mean like Nate Maggard and his bunch," Johnny said with such an innocent tone, his father gave him a knifing look.

"You just never mind about Nate Maggard. He's nothing but trash." Bill blew on his coffee, sending ripples across the surface, and shredding the steam that still rose from the hot liquid.

"Then how come you been playing cards with him at the tavern, Papa?"

"Let's talk about Willis. Why did you get into a fight with him?"

"He called me an orphan and a bastard."

"Well, you're not an orphan and you're not a bastard either. I'm your papa and everybody knows that."

"It wasn't just Willis. There was a whole bunch of boys ragging me."

"They're just jealous, that's all."

"They said they were going to kill me," Johnny said.

"Kill you?"

"Yes, sir. I told 'em to come ahead."

"Well, you made a mistake there, son. When you got a bunch together, they don't have no brains among 'em. It's just one blind brain doin' all the thinkin'. That's when you got to get out and go. Ride to the sunset."

"You're always sayin' that, Papa. What does that mean?"

"It means save your ass. When you're outnumbered, no matter if you're in the right, you just head west, son. Ride to the setting sun and don't stop until it goes down."

"Is that what you did, Papa?"

Bill gulped a mouthful of coffee, swallowed it. Tears welled up in his eyes. "Too hot," he said, blinking to clear his eyes of moisture.

"When you left Kentucky, I mean," Johnny said.

"You were just a tadpole then."

"I know. But Mama told me the story many times."

"The way she told it warn't the way it was."

"But you never talked about it, Papa."

"With good reason. Ain't worth tellin' no way."

"You kilt a man, though, didn't you? More'n one, the way Mama told it."

"It's not something I'm right proud of," Bill said.

"You was in the right, though. Were in the right, I mean."

"Bein' in the right didn't make it no better, Johnny. Folks back there, back then, didn't care that I was in the right. I had to ride to the sunset, taking you and your mama with me."

"And that old mule, Petey."

Bill laughed. "Yeah, Petey come with us, and two horses I owned. You rode with your mama and we kept ridin' over the Natchez Trace and clear up to St. Louis."

"And then we came here."

"Johnny, maybe you better go back to studyin' that book and leave me be with all that. Then you gotta go to work at the mercantile. And don't be late no more. What's past is done past and we can't go back there no more."

"You mean back to Kentucky."

"I mean back to wherever we was back then. Now go

on. I'll take my cup to the shop with me once I fill it up
again and I don't want to see you until supper time."

"Yes, Papa."

"And I mean don't you go down to the docks and don't
you get in no trouble. And you'd better shuck yourself of
that pistol. It might get you into trouble."

"Yes, sir," Johnny said, taking off his pistol and picking
up his book. He set his coffee cup on the sideboard and
left his father sitting alone at the table, drinking his coffee,
staring at the pistol he had made for his son.

He knew of a place he could go where nobody would
bother him, but it was a long walk and he'd have to go
to work at the mercantile in Sibley at nine o'clock sharp.
He'd be hungry long before Old Man Whitaker let him
off for lunch. The widow woman would bring Papa his
lunch at the blacksmith shop. She always did. She had
her eyes set on Papa now that he was a widower and soon
to have a son grown and gone from the house.

The only thing was, she was the mother of Willis and
he was as bad as they come. He might have a black eye
right now, but he deserved worse, and Johnny just hoped
he wouldn't run into him anytime during the day.

And he couldn't stand Willis's mother. She was a witch
and didn't deserve his father. She had already worn out
one husband and now she wanted to wear out another.

3

HE KNEW THE TIDES AND THE RIPPLES AND THE SWIRLS, the undertow of the muscular Missouri River as it flowed past Fort Osage and the settlement of Sibley, named after the first factor, George Sibley. He knew the river's tide pools, and from its colors, the seasons of the year. But Johnny did not know where the river came from, even though he knew it was wending its mysterious and mighty way to the sea.

The river never failed to fascinate him. He could sit on its banks and watch it for hours, counting the bugs and insects that had drowned in its murky waters, wondering about the sticks and grasses that floated past him, and the logs, gently rolling over and over as the river pulled them past his lookout point. Sometimes he would see a drowned muskrat or a beaver caught in the flow, and he would wonder what had killed them and how far they had come.

He knew the river at night when the moon painted its ripples silver and nested in its waves or striped it with a shimmering light. Those nights when he walked to the river to be alone, to dream while waking, he became more aware of the immense secrets hidden in the depths of the

Missouri, and he could feel its powerful pull on him, the
way the moon would rise and make the river dance to its
silent music. He would sit for hours, lost in the magic of
the night and the soft sighing of the river, and his father
would have to call him home, his voice carrying clear and
gruff on the still night air.

Now Johnny watched the sun rise, calculating the time
he had left on the river before he had to go Whitaker's
Mercantile and start work. There was time, and he cracked
open the book and began to read where he left off. Soon
he became lost in the story of Ulysses, the words flowing
through him like the breeze through his dark hair, and as
always, the words set up a tingling as the hairs on the
back of his neck rose. His empty belly swirled with moths
at each thrilling sentence.

Johnny heard a sound and turned away from his book.
His mouth opened wide as he saw Willis and some other
boys heading toward him. For a moment, he froze in surprise, then stood up. He could tell by the way Willis
walked that he had blood in his eye, and the other boys
bore expressions that made clear their intent.

"Whatcha doin', Stagg?" Willis said. "Readin' one of
them fancy books?"

"What do you want, Willis?"

"Oh, nothin'. Just wanted to see what you were doin'."

Willis squared off in front of Johnny while the other
boys made a circle. Johnny knew one or two of them from
school. Scott Lamb was one, Eric Nordstrum another. Eric
stooped down and picked up the book Johnny had been
reading.

"Give me that," Johnny said, reaching for the book.

Nordstrum jerked the book away, opened it up, and spat
into it.

"You bastard," Johnny said, reaching out again to grab
the book from the boy.

"That book ain't nothin' but ass paper," Willis said.

"And we've all got to take a shit. Give us each some pages, Eric."

"Don't," Johnny said.

Nordstrum grinned and started ripping pages out of the book and handing them to the other boys. Johnny went after him, his fists balled up. He struck out, then felt a powerful blow to his right cheekbone as Willis hauled off and smashed a fist into him with full force.

Johnny staggered sideways, his head surging with pain, his ear ringing as the pain spread. He turned to face his attacker, but the other boys swarmed over him and he felt fists pounding into his mouth and chest and belly.

Then the boys were all yelling insults at him and smashing him with their fists so hard he fell down. Before he could get up, Willis began kicking him in the side. Nordstrum kicked him in the genitals and Johnny screamed. Blood poured from his lips and his vision blurred. Another boy kicked him in the head, and the sky started to whirl around before it turned black. He felt himself sinking deep into a dark bottomless pit, and then he could no longer hear anything. After a moment, even the pain went away as he fell unconscious.

He remembered crying out just before everything went black in his mind, but he didn't know what he had said until he woke up sometime later to a pain that gripped him like a steel vise. He felt like one huge boil, like something that had been dipped into his father's blazing forge. Every muscle, ever fiber in his body pulsed and throbbed in agony.

He knew that every bone in his body must be broken. He knew that every muscle had been smashed, squashed beyond recognition. He knew that he was covered with blood and that he was dying.

He called out again, and that was when he remembered what he had screamed before he had passed out. "Mama," he cried. And then the tears came, and his body shook all

over as he realized he was not dead and that his bones
were not broken and his flesh not mashed into pulp like
a squashed tomato. But the goddamned pain, he thought,
the goddamned pain was beyond bearing. Beyond mortal
endurance.

Johnny tried to sit up, and it felt as if he was weighted
down with a hundredweight of pig iron. Pain shot through
him like lightning bolts, into every crevice and cranny,
piercing his brain like a sharp knife.

"Oh, Mama, goddamn," Johnny cried, and felt ashamed
of himself. He wrenched himself off the ground to a sitting position and gulped in air to stop himself from sobbing. His lungs felt as if they had been burned inside. The
air burned like fire, and he felt his ribs to see if they were
broken. As if he could tell, he thought. They felt broken.
It hurt like hell to breathe. He felt his face, around his
eyes where it hurt so much, and his fingertips slid gingerly
over swollen lumps that ballooned over each eye. His lips
were puffy, cracked, clogged with dried blood. But there
was no blood on his trousers, and only a little smattering
on his shirt. The sun hurt his swollen eyes, and he crawled
until he could stand. His legs were wobbly, but he was
on his feet and when he saw where the sun was, it felt as
if a hand had squeezed his heart. It was not low in the
sky, but high overhead, past noon, he figured, and blazing
like hellfire itself.

"Jesus," he said, and it was as much a prayer as it was
a curse on his bloated lips.

Pages of the torn-up book lay scattered about, some of
them flapping in the breeze, others tumbling from one
clump of dirt to another, and some were stuck to the sage
and grasses that grew along the riverbank.

Johnny swayed there in pain and disbelief, tears streaming down his battered face. He set out to pick up the
scattered pages, pain shooting through him like hot jave-
lins. He groaned when he stooped over to pick up a scrap.

The leather binding lay among some stones, and he picked it up and began stuffing pages inside as he wandered through the wasteland of *The Odyssey*'s decimated innards.

He saw where the boys had defecated and used pages from his book to wipe themselves, and he muttered under his breath every curse word he knew. He looked all around finally, and saw no more pages lying on the ground, and started walking toward town in a stagger, every step a long journey through a tortuous garden of pure agony.

He appeared at the front of the mercantile store sometime later, aching in every bone and joint, his entire body feeling like a raw wound. Mr. Whitaker, responding to the whispers and hushed voices of patrons outside and inside his store, walked out on the porch and looked down at the disheveled Johnny Stagg, the man's arms akimbo, a dark scowl on his face.

"Do you know what time it is, Johnny?"

"No, sir."

"It's well past noon and we had two boats and three wagons come in this morning."

"I—I'm sorry, Mr. Whitaker, I—I, uh . . ."

"And look at you. That's no way to show up for work."

"No, sir. I, uh . . ."

"You can pick up your pay in the morning or after work today. I won't tolerate a slacker."

"But I . . ."

Whitaker turned on his heel and went back inside the store. The people outside on the boardwalk started to snicker, and a couple of men gave him dirty looks. Johnny turned around and walked away, clutching what was left of his book to his side. He tried not to listen to what the people were saying. He felt humiliated and scorned by the entire town.

By the time Johnny reached home, his pains were so

severe that he forgot all about hunger. He dipped into the bucket on the sideboard and drank water until his stomach started to churn. Then he walked like a wooden man into his bedroom and eased himself onto his bed. He dropped the torn and ripped book to the floor and lay down on his back.

He lay there, one arm across his eyes to shut out the light, and tried to quell his anger and the pain that wracked his body. Finally he fell asleep, and the pain receded and wound itself like a coiling serpent into his dreams.

Johnny did not know how long he had slept, but when he opened his eyes, the sun had gone down. A moment later, he realized what had awakened him, a noise at the front door, a soft tapping that felt like someone hammering tenpenny nails into his head.

"Johnny, me boy."

"Paddy?" Johnny's voice was a croak in his throat.

"Are ye awake, Johnny-boy?"

"Come on in, Paddy." This time his voice was louder, less froggy.

"Sure, and the door is open, but I didn't know was I welcome. Where are ye, Johnny?"

"In here. In bed."

The house was dark. Paddy had not been there but once before, and only then in the front room. Johnny heard him crash into a chair, then a table. Finally, Johnny saw a dark shadow at his doorway.

"There ye are," Paddy said. "Sleepin', were ye?"

"Leave me alone, Paddy."

"Not till you hear what I have to say. Can you light a lamp?"

"No. What do you want?"

"You'd better get down to the tavern, Johnny-boy. There's bound to be trouble."

"Trouble? What trouble?"

"Your pa's playin' cards and winnin' and there's grumbling from the losers at the table."

"There's always trouble when Papa wins at cards. It doesn't mean much."

"There's somethin' funny goin' on. I don't like the looks of it."

"What can I do? If Papa wants to play cards, I can't stop him."

Paddy walked over to the lamp and found the lucifers. He struck one, lifted the glass chimney, and lit the wick. Then he turned up the wick after dropping the chimney. The room glowed with an orange light.

"Lord, Johnny," Paddy said. "You look like you've been stung by hornets."

Johnny turned away from the glare of the lamp.

"What happened to ye?" Paddy asked. He looked down at the floor and saw the remnants of the book, the flotsam of papers, the wrecked binding. He stooped over and picked up the book and most of the pages.

"Sad way to treat a book," Paddy said.

"Just put it down, Paddy."

"I think Nate Maggard's going to pick a fight with your daddy," Paddy said.

"What makes you think that?"

"He's makin' remarks and grumblin'. I think you ought to go over there and see for yourself."

"I don't feel good," Johnny said.

"I wouldn't have come over here if I didn't think it was important, Johnny-boy."

"Papa can take care of himself."

"If it was just Maggard, maybe. But there's some ugly characters in the saloon tonight."

Johnny sighed and got up from the bed. He ached all over, but he knew Paddy wouldn't have come by unless he was worried about Johnny's father. Nate Maggard was a no-good lout, and Johnny didn't know why his father would play cards with such a man. Nate had beaten a man half to death a year or so ago, so Johnny knew he had a temper. And he was mean, by anybody's standards.

"All right. I haven't eaten and I'm pretty stove up, but I'll go over to the saloon with you."

"Good boy. I know your pa will appreciate it."

"I doubt it. I guess he didn't come home when he finished work."

"No, he went right to the saloon."

"And you went with him," Johnny said.

"Well, he did offer to buy me a drink."

Johnny threw water on his face. He didn't look at himself in the mirror. He felt very bad, and he knew he must look even worse. On the way out, he strapped on his pistol and checked the pan. He slipped on his possible pouch, which contained a powder horn, extra flints, cloth patches, bear grease, and lead balls.

"Good idea," Paddy said. "You can give it to your papa if he needs it."

"What? The pistol?"

"Yes," Paddy said. "He's not armed."

"Well, this is my pistol and I aim to hang onto it."

"Oh, a bluff, right?"

Johnny blew out the lamp and looked at Paddy in the darkness.

"It's no bluff, Paddy. I know how to use it. Papa taught me. If anyone tries to beat him up, I'll use it."

"Those are mighty brave words from a boy what ain't blooded himself yet. Didn't your pa tell you?"

"Tell me what?"

"If you draw that pistol, you'd better be damned ready to use it."

"He told me," Johnny said. "And if I draw it, I'll sure as hell be ready to use it."

"You could kill a man, Johnny?"

"I don't know," Johnny said. "I guess it would depend on how mad I was."

The two walked out the door and into the night.

"The ones I seen getting' mad and drawin' pistols was the ones who got killed first," said Paddy.

"Let's hope I don't have to use it," Johnny said.

And he meant it.

4

JOHNNY LOOKED AT THE SKY, SNIFFED THE NIGHT AIR. He could smell the river in its nocturnal silence. The air was thick with the cloying scents of the barges and bull boats at anchor, and the sky was heavy with clouds. He could smell rain, too, far off perhaps, but on the river, the weather could change at any minute.

The town of Sibley was dark except for the few windows glowing orange and yellow with lamplight. The road was empty, and it seemed to him as if the universe had paused for a breath and plunged the earth into a sudden silence.

"You better go on home, Paddy," Johnny said.

"Oh, I wouldn't miss this for anything."

"Miss what? There isn't going to be any trouble."

"I can sniff it in the air, Johnny."

"You're smelling your upper lip, Paddy, and that's whiskey you're sniffing."

"You've got the sharp tongue, like your mother, Pauline, bless her sweet German soul. But I seen the glint in Nate Maggard's eye, and Phill Hardesty, he give me a sign like he knows there's going to be trouble."

"Phill Hardesty is scairt of his own shadow."

"Hardesty probably knows what goes on in this town more'n anybody 'ceptin' the barber. He hears it all, sees it all."

"And blabs it all," Johnny said, but as they neared the main street of Sibley, he felt a growing apprehension. There was nothing he could put his finger on, but he felt as if something was wrong. Maybe it wasn't something connected to his pa at all. Maybe it had to do with Whitaker firing him, or getting beaten up. Or maybe it had something to do with his book being ruined by those same boys.

As he and Paddy drew in sight of Verdun's Tavern, Johnny knew that something was wrong. It was too quiet. There wasn't a soul on the street, and he thought he could hear muffled sounds coming from the tavern.

"Paddy," Johnny whispered. "Where is everybody? Shouldn't there be people about?"

"I dunno. Maybe. It's awful quiet. Maybe the trouble went away."

"I don't think so." Johnny approached the tavern and heard sounds he could not identify. And the light from inside was blocked by something, or someone. The boardwalk was almost totally dark, and he knew that wasn't right.

When Johnny stepped inside the saloon, it took him a moment to pry his way through a crowd of men. The tavern was filled with nearly two dozen men and they were all looking at one thing.

"Uh-oh, Nate, here comes the pup," someone said.

Johnny stiffened and muscled his way through the outer ring of spectators. The crowd parted to let him through.

What Johnny saw next, he would never forget as long as he lived.

Bill Stagg was kneeling on the floor, his arms up as shields over his face. Nate Maggard stood over him, a pistol in his hand, slashing at Johnny's father with the barrel. Bill's face and arms were streaked with blood.

Nate stopped and looked up at Johnny. Then he made a lopsided grin and brought the pistol down, butt-first, and smashed Bill on the top of the head. Bill made a sound and slumped over, blood gushing from his skull.

"Stop," Johnny yelled.

Nate looked at Johnny again and turned away as Bill struggled and began to rise up from the floor.

A deep hush invaded the room and heads turned to look at Johnny. Someone let out a sigh. Paddy sniffled.

"Stay out of this, kid," Nate said.

"You leave my father alone," Johnny said.

"Kid, I'm tellin' you. Mind your own business."

Johnny did not move. He stood there, glaring at Maggard, a broad-chested man with burly shoulders, thick arms and wrists, powerful of build, though short in stature. He was the kind of man others stood aside for to let him pass, with a jaw that jutted out belligerently and dark porcine eyes so brown they looked black.

Maggard hesitated for a moment, as if he could not believe that Johnny was still standing there, had not left. He shifted the pistol in his hand to get a better grip on the butt.

"Johnny," Paddy whispered behind him, "you best back away from this one. Nate means to kill you."

Johnny said nothing.

"Well, kid," Maggard said, "if that's the way you want it, I guess I don't have much choice."

Maggard, sure of himself, swung his pistol to bear on Johnny. In those scant seconds, many of those there felt it took an eternity for Maggard to aim and cock his pistol. And in that eternity lurked the pale face of death, and every man in the room felt it, and some even said later that they saw it as a wraith in the smoke that spewed from the barrel of a pistol.

But in that frozen second, or seconds, or instant,

Johnny's hand flew to the butt of his pistol, and his hand was a blur of speed that left many a witness dumbfounded until the end of his days.

Johnny drew his pistol and cocked it even as it came to level, the barrel pointed at Maggard's belly like the hideous snout of a deadly snake. Some saw Johnny's finger squeeze the trigger, but that was perhaps only an illusion, a trick of the mind, a chemical spasm in the brain that filled in blanks with memory or speculation.

But they all saw Johnny's small-caliber pistol buck in his hand, saw bright orange flame blossom from the muzzle, followed by a cloud of white smoke. Some heard the flint strike the plate and heard the hiss of black powder ignite and shoot through the touch hole into the magazine, where it ignited the main charge of twelve or fifteen grains of powder nestled beneath a patch of rough cloth and a round lead ball.

Some even saw Maggard's mouth drop open, and others heard the sudden rush of air from his lungs that produced a harsh sound in his throat that emerged as a kind of grunt.

Maggard stumbled backward, his own bloody pistol, a huge-bored weapon with a nine-inch barrel, tumbling from his hand. A chunk of his backbone blew out from his spine. It sounded like a dry limb cracking underfoot of something very large and heavy. And blood burst from a wound above Maggard's belt buckle and sprayed those nearby, before it began to dribble down the front of Maggard's trousers as his knees buckled and he sank to the floor.

"My God, he killed him," someone gasped, and men who had ducked just before Johnny fired his pistol lifted their heads to see if this was true.

Johnny holstered his pistol and ran over to his father. He turned him over and lifted his head and shoulders, cradled them in his arms. He bent his head to his father's mouth and felt breath on his cheek.

"Papa," Johnny said. "Papa?"

"Son," his father breathed.

"Don't die, Papa. Please don't die."

Tears welled up in Johnny's eyes as he held his father close to him. His father's eyes opened and Johnny saw the pain in them. He wiped some of the blood from his father's forehead, and the tears in his eyes spilled over and ran down his cheeks.

"I'm goin', Johnny," Bill said. "Mind what I told you."

"Don't go, Papa."

"Ride," his father said. His voice was weak.

"Huh? Papa?"

"Always . . ."

"Papa, stay with me. Please."

"Ride to the sunset."

Johnny heard the words plainly. He had heard them before, but they tore at his heart as they never had before. His father let out a deep sigh and then was still. Those were the last words Johnny would ever hear from his father.

Paddy knelt down beside Johnny. He put a hand on the young man's shoulder. Then he crossed himself with his right hand. "He's gone, Johnny-boy. Your pa's gone."

"I know," Johnny sobbed. "Damn it, I know. . . ."

"No man here will speak against you, Johnny," Paddy said. He looked up at the men gazing down on them. "Ain't that right?" Paddy said to them, one and all.

"It was self-defense," one man ventured.

"Maggard threw down on him," the bartender, Phill Hardesty, said in a loud voice. "You all saw it. Nate killed Bill Stagg and then was going to kill young Johnny here."

There was a murmur of voices, all assenting to Hardesty's proclamation.

"Bill there was cheating at cards," one man said, and everyone grew silent.

"Who said that?" Hardesty asked, his tone stern and hard.

"I mean, that's what Nate said."

"Nate was a goddamned liar," another man said, and the voices rose up again until Paddy held up his hand.

"Anyone who ever watched Bill play or played with him at a game of cards knew he never cheated. Bill Stagg was as honest as the day is long, and I'll brook no man here saying any different."

"I'll back that," Hardesty said. "Bill Stagg was an honest man."

Paddy stood up. Johnny was too wracked with grief to move or say anything. He kept looking at his father's bloody face. Bill's eyes were still open, glazed with the frost of death. Johnny touched each one and closed the lids. He choked back the sobs that threatened to break loose, and he swallowed saliva into a dry throat that seemed paralyzed at that moment of death.

"Anybody who don't have business here, clear out," Hardesty said in a loud voice. "Some of you take Nate down to the undertaker's. The rest of you, go on home. The bar is closed."

The men in the tavern milled around and most of them left. Four men lifted Nate's body up by his legs and arms. One of them looked at Johnny and said: "Sonny, I'm real sorry about your pa gittin' hisself killed. But was I you, I'd put some distance 'twixt Sibley and you. Nate Maggard's got kin and they ain't goin' to like this none. No matter who was right."

Johnny looked at the man, but did not recognize him. Johnny nodded and watched as the men carried Maggard's body out of the saloon. The batwing doors swung on leather hinges and made a sorrowful sound.

When the doors stopped swinging, it was very quiet in

the saloon. Phill Hardesty still stood behind the bar, and there was one other man down at the far end, his face shaded by his hat.

"Whit, you stayin'?" Hardesty asked the man in shadow.

"No, I'm leaving, Phill. I just want to settle up with Johnny before I go."

Johnny recognized the voice. It was Vern Whitaker, the man who had fired him that afternoon. Whitaker downed the rest of his drink and walked up to Johnny.

"Here's what I owe you, Johnny. You don't need to come by the store."

He handed Johnny a sheaf of bills and some coins. Johnny didn't count the money, but slid it into his pocket.

"Thanks, Mr. Whitaker."

"I feel sorry for you, kid, but you're nothing but trouble and so was your pappy."

"You've said enough, Whit," Hardesty said from behind the bar. "Take your leave."

Whitaker took one last look at Bill Stagg and then walked out of the saloon. Paddy spat into the sawdust on the floor as the batwings swung.

"Man can't say nothin' good about someone who's passed on, he ought to keep his mouth shut," Paddy said.

"Johnny, I'll buy you and Paddy a drink before I close up," said Phill, "We'll help you carry your pa off to wherever you need to go."

Johnny nodded, feeling numb inside and out.

He looked down at the battered face and head of his father. His father had been battered mercilessly by Nate Maggard. His skull was smashed in a couple of places, the blood already dried. What kind of a bastard would pistol-whip a man to death? he wondered.

Johnny rubbed the wounds tenderly with the tip of his finger as if trying to smooth them away. His heart felt as if it was caught in his throat. He thought of his father that morning, when they had drunk coffee together. He had seemed so alive, so robust, so full of energy, and now, there was nothing left of him. There was only a shell, a shape that had once been his father, but now no longer breathed, no longer spoke, nor laughed. And there was no reason now for him to be dead.

His mother, Pauline, had died of the lung disease and she had been frail for a long time. While it was a shock to him and his father when she died, they knew there was a reason she had died. They knew she had been sick.

But with Johnny's father, there had been no warning, no sickness to take him from life. Instead, a savage man had taken the breath of his father away, had consigned him to a grave without warning. His father, Johnny knew, had died before his time.

"Where do you want to take your pa, Johnny?" Paddy asked, his voice soft, almost a whisper. "I can help you wash him, change his clothes."

"Huh?" Johnny came out of his reverie with Paddy's words, but he was still lost, floating outside himself like a boat without an anchor.

"Bill has to be taken care of," Hardesty said. "We'll help you carry him somewheres where you can clean him up, make him proper for burying."

"Oh. I guess we should take him over to Mrs. Coombs. She'll want to know and she took care of my mama when she . . ."

"Yes, I think that's a good idea, Johnny," Paddy said. "Phill and I will carry him. You go on over and tell Mrs. Coombs we're coming."

"Yes," Johnny said, shaking his head as if to clear his mind. He stood up, like a man in a trance, and looked around. Then he looked back down at his father. He began to weep again, but he held back, knowing that there would be more grief to come and he didn't want to show Paddy and Phill how weak he was, how terribly lost he felt.

"You go on, Johnny," Phill said. "We'll be there at Mrs. Coombs's directly."

"All right." Johnny started to walk away, then saw Maggard's pistol still lying on the floor. He walked over to it and picked it up. Nate hadn't even had time to cock it. The pistol was heavy in his hand. The bore looked to be at least .60-caliber. Such a pistol would knock a man down, would blow a big hole in him. He drew in a breath and stuck the pistol in his belt. Then he walked toward the door.

He stopped and turned around, looked at Phill and Paddy.

"I'm not running," he said. "I'm not afraid of those damned Maggards."

Then he pushed through the batwing doors and out into the night. Somehow, he felt taller at that moment, and a great deal older.

5

JOHNNY WALKED DOWN THE DARK STREETS OF SIBLEY to Mrs. Coombs's house. It was at the end of Laurel Street, a small building that, like so many others, still showed its lineage. It was part log cabin, part planed lumber, small-looking from the outside, but big enough inside for two people. There was a little picket fence around it that his father had built after Lucille Coombs had lost her husband, and a gate. Flowers bloomed along the fence and around the house; pansies and morning glories and some honeysuckle. There were some small trees, a couple of box elders and some young oaks that he and his father had planted in the past year, sent upriver from St. Charles.

Johnny walked through the gate. It didn't creak like so many others in town, thanks to his father's expert workmanship and maintenance. It made only a small sound when he opened and closed it. He walked up on the porch and tapped on the door.

For several seconds, Johnny heard no sound, and then he heard a rustling from inside. Then he heard footsteps, getting louder and louder.

"Who is it?" Mrs. Coombs called through the latched door.

"It's me, Mrs. Coombs. Johnny Stagg."

"Who?" Her voice sounded sleepy, Johnny thought.

He told her his name again.

"Johnny? Is that you?"

"Yes, Mrs. Coombs. I have to talk to you."

"Is your daddy with you?"

"No, ma'am. Please. Open the door."

"Wait'll I light the lamp," she said, her voice muffled behind the door.

Johnny waited. He heard her fumbling around in the dark and then he heard a match striking. A few seconds later, he saw a feeble light through the front-room window. Moments later, the door opened and Mrs. Coombs stood there, wearing a nightcap and a robe. Her feet were encased in purple slippers. She looked, Johnny thought, a hundred years old.

"Come in, Johnny," she said. "Where's Bill?"

"Let's sit down, can we, Mrs. Coombs?"

"Lordy, what time is it? Heavens, it must be near midnight."

"No, ma'am, it's not even ten o'clock."

"Well, sit down. Over there on the divan. What brings you over here so late? And where is your father? Why are you carrying those guns? Is something wrong?"

Slowly, painfully, Johnny told her what happened to his father, but he didn't tell her that he had killed Nate Maggard. She had enough to handle without dealing with that right then.

Mrs. Coombs buried her face in her hands while Johnny sat there, feeling uncomfortable. He listened to her sobs and knew she had deep feelings for his father. It was hard to watch someone else grieving. He felt so helpless. He couldn't even handle his own grief, much less hers, just then.

Finally, Mrs. Coombs took a deep breath and lifted her head. She looked at Johnny with tear-filled eyes. Then she took a hanky from her sleeve and dried the tears from her cheeks.

"Where is your father now, Johnny? You didn't just leave him there in that smelly saloon, did you?"

"Mr. Hardesty and Paddy Osteen are bringing Papa over here. I was wondering if you would . . ."

"Bathe your father like I did your mother? Johnny, you don't have to ask."

"He—he looks pretty bad, Mrs. Coombs."

"I wish you'd call me Lucy, like your father did. I'm so sorry, Johnny. I hope justice will be done. It's so sad."

"Yes'm."

"Well, now," she said, "there's no use you waiting around here and getting in the way. I want you to run home and pick out your father's best clothes. Bring me his good shoes, be sure they're shined up real pretty, clean underwear if he has any, and he should. I just washed his things a day or so ago, a nice clean shirt, his best trousers, and a tie. Bring the nice clothes he would wear to church and I'll dress him up right nice."

"Papa didn't go to church, Mrs. Coombs."

"Well, never mind. Just go and bring what I'll need. Don't you worry about your father. I'll wash him real good so he'll look nice at the funeral and when he meets his maker."

"Yes'm."

Johnny got up in a daze. It was all happening so fast. There was so much to do and he felt all thumbs. He was glad Mrs. Coombs was taking care of some of the things.

"You come back in about an hour, Johnny. You don't have to knock. Just come right on in."

"Yes'm." Johnny left quickly and started running to his house. He slowed when he realized it was more than a mile away. He was glad he had something to do. It took his mind off what had happened. He could hardly believe any of it.

When he arrived at his house, he half expected his father to be there. When he went inside, though, he knew that was only wishful thinking. His papa was gone and he'd never be in his house again.

Johnny's footsteps echoed in the empty house. Funny, he thought, he'd never noticed them before. Now, they sounded loud and hollow, and he felt a tightening in his chest that was something like fear. Fear of what? Of his father's ghost? His mother's? He lit a lamp with shaking fingers, turned up the wick, and stood there in the orange glow. The light produced shadows in the room, and the shadows seemed to take on eerie shapes. Human shapes. Ghostly shapes.

"Hey," he said aloud. "Anybody here?" He knew he was alone, but he needed the bravery of his own words so that he could walk away from the lamp and the light and do what he had come to do.

Johnny walked into his father's room, carrying the lamp in his hand. More shadows, more dark shapes. He set the lamp on his father's chest of drawers and went first to the wardrobe. It was funny then, because he remembered how he used to go in there and try on his father's shoes, which were always too big for him. But he would put them on and clump around the room when nobody was there to watch his silliness.

Now, there was a sadness when he looked at his father's shoes, the good pair. They were shined, because his father kept them that way, and he picked them up and set them by the bed. It was hard then to hold back the tears, but he fought them down and went back to the closet.

He set out a pair of pants and his father's good coat. He found underwear in the drawer, and socks. He smelled them and they held the scent of lye soap, very faint, but stronger when he drew air through his nostrils. Mrs. Coombs did their laundry, but that was another thing he had seldom noticed—that odd clean smell that clung to their clothing when Mrs. Coombs brought them back over after washing.

For luck, Johnny found the new pair of galluses he had bought his father and which he had worn only once. He laid the suspenders out with the other clothes, and then returned to his father's bedroom and slid out the box under the bed. The forbidden box. His heart began pounding as he opened it and gazed down at the fine pistol that lay in a bed of crimson satin. He had only seen the pistol a few times when his father had brought it out to clean and oil it.

The pistol was a graceful flintlock, the stock made of rosewood. The lock was imported from England, and a gunsmith in Kentucky had made the pistol for his father. The barrel was of the finest Damascus steel, bored to .50-caliber so it would match the bore on his father's rifle, made in Lancaster County, Kentucky, by a German gunsmith named Karl Kruger for Bill's father, Johnny's grandfather, Anthony Stagg.

Johnny picked up the pistol, held it gently in his hand. He turned it over so the lamplight would catch it, and saw the S carved into the checkered grip, just like the S on the Kentucky rifle that stood in a corner of the wardrobe. The pistol and rifle were almost a matching set, except the stock of the rifle was made of beautiful curly maple. But that S carved in the stock was almost an exact match, and both of the barrels were finely browned, both had English locks, and both were .50-caliber weapons.

There was a buckskin sheath with long fringes for the rifle, just like the mountain men carried. There was a box of hard velvet flints, too, and a possibles pouch, and powder horn. The pistol came with a brass powder flask that was etched with hunting scenes: a large stag, a wild boar, and a turkey in full strut with flared tail and long beard.

Somewhere, too, among his father's things, Johnny knew, there was a fine holster for the pistol, and his father always kept it supple and shined with bear grease, and there was a tin of that in the possibles pouch, along with patches and plenty of lead balls and a mold.

Johnny sighed and put the pistol back in the wooden box, closed it, and pushed it back under the bed. But his heart was pounding, and he could almost feel his father's presence in the room.

When Johnny had finished gathering his father's clothes, he carried the lamp into the kitchen and sat down at the table. He looked at the pistol that Nate Maggard had used to kill his father. The barrel was smeared with blood and strands of his father's hair. Johnny's stomach turned, and he had to fight down the bile that rose up in his throat. He turned the pistol over and over in his hand, and it seemed to grow heavier and uglier the more he looked at it. He wanted to run down to the river and throw it in, but sensibility overcame his anger and revulsion. It was a fine pistol and he would keep it, if not to use, then as a reminder of what a bad man had used to kill his good father.

Johnny walked into his room and shoved the pistol under his pillow. Then he sat down at the kitchen table and cleaned the black powder residue from the barrel of his own pistol. He did this quickly, knowing he could give it a more thorough cleaning later. He reloaded the pistol, seated the lead ball, and poured a thin patina of powder onto the pan and blew away the surplus. He made sure the flint was tight and that it would strike the plate should he need to shoot it again. He holstered the pistol and stood up, took in a deep breath.

He carefully stacked his father's clothes and set the shoes on top, then blew out the lamp and left the house.

When he retuned to Mrs. Coombs's, he saw the empty wagon parked out front and knew Paddy and Phill were there with his father's body. For a moment he dreaded going in and seeing his father's corpse again. When he walked up to the door and started to open it, he was startled when Paddy pushed it open and reached out to him.

"I'll take those, Johnny. Mrs. Coombs will need them directly."

Before Johnny could say anything, Paddy took the pile from Johnny and Phill stepped out onto the porch, blocking Johnny from going in.

"Maybe you and I should talk some before you go in there, Johnny," Hardesty said. "Besides, Lucy's pretty busy right now."

"How come I can't go in now?" Johnny asked.

"Oh, you can, you can, Johnny. But I think this would be a good time for you and me to have a little talk. Besides, there's nothing you can do in there. Lucy and Paddy will fix your pa up and then you can see him, maybe say good-bye to him."

Hardesty took Johnny by the arm and led him off the porch and off to the side of the house, where it was dark and private.

"There's something you ought to know, Johnny," Hardesty said. "I figured it out when Nate was pistol-whipping your pa, but just now I was able to confirm what I saw and what I suspicioned about over at the saloon."

"What's that?" Johnny asked.

"Before Nate Maggard took the gun to your pa, there was another man who set your pa up. Poor Bill didn't have a chance."

"What do you mean, this man set my papa up?"

"He shoved an Arkansas toothpick in your pa's back, clear up to the hilt, and then lit a shuck."

"You mean my papa was knifed first? Before Nate clubbed him with his pistol?"

"Yeah. I just saw the wound. It happened real quick, and I just caught a glimpse of the knife and the man shoving the blade into Bill's back. It was real quick."

"My God," Johnny said.

"Him and Nate set Bill up, that's for sure, and if you're looking for that strongbox your pa kept here at Mrs. Coombs', it ain't there."

"Papa kept all his money there, I know," Johnny said. "There was gold and notes and silver."

"I know. I just finished talking to Lucy about it. She said Nate came over late this afternoon with a note from Bill asking her to give him the strongbox. Said he needed it real bad."

"And Mrs. Coombs believed him?"

"She said he had a note and it looked like Bill's handwriting. She just remembered it, and now she's real sorry."

"That note was a damned forgery."

"I know, Johnny. Nate got your pa into a card game because he didn't want anyone to know about that money."

"Why, hell, there must have been hundreds of dollars Papa had saved up to buy us a ranch out West."

Phill hung his head. "I know, I know. Bill himself told me it was a goodly sum, more than two thousand dollars."

"How do you come to know about it?" Johnny asked.

"Bill wanted me to know. He said if anything ever happened to him, you was to have it. I reckon Nate, or someone, must have overheard us talking about it."

"Mrs. Coombs never should have given that money to Haggard."

"Don't be too hard on her, Johnny. She's old and addled and you can't hold her responsible. I reckon, from what she told me, that Nate told her some cock-and-bull story and she showed him where she kept the strongbox, then gave it to him. She didn't even know what was in it."

"No, I know she didn't, because Papa told me he didn't tell her. Just asked her to hold on to it until he needed it."

"She thought it was property papers, a deed and the like," Hardesty said.

"So where is the strongbox now? You suppose Nate hid it somewhere? And if he didn't, who has it?"

"I oughten not to tell you, Johnny."

"Why not?"

"Because," Hardesty said, "the knowledge could get you killed."

Johnny drew in a breath. Anger blazed in him like a sudden storm coming onto the plains from nowhere. He wanted to strike out, to shake Hardesty and hit someone. Anyone.

A great bitterness began to build in Johnny's heart. There was so much he didn't know about why his father was murdered, and it looked like Phill wasn't going to tell him.

Johnny balled up his fists and lunged toward Hardesty, blind with that sudden, overpowering rage that had risen up in him at the injustice and treachery surrounding his father's murder.

At that moment, Johnny was not thinking clearly and he was about to make the biggest mistake of his life. But he was blinded by a rage and bitterness that had smothered his grief as quickly as a fingertip snuffs out a candle.

6

PHILL TOOK A STEP BACK AS JOHNNY LUNGED TOWARD him. Then he brought up his arms and grabbed Johnny at the elbows, preventing him from striking out with both fists.

"Damn you, Phill," Johnny raged, "you're in it with them. You're just like them."

"What in hell's got into you, Johnny? I ain't like them. I'm on your side."

"Well, you don't act like it. You'd better tell me who stuck that blade in my papa's back or I'll beat you to a bloody pulp."

"Johnny, hold on." Hardesty pushed his arms out straight to keep Johnny from swinging at him again. "You'd better listen to me."

"Well, go on ahead then, but I want to know who murdered my papa."

"Johnny, that man who stuck your daddy is a hard man and far meaner than Nate Maggard. Fact is, I think he meant to kill Nate over your pa's money if you hadn't done it first."

"I want the bastard's name," Johnny said, his eyes blazing with a fury that Hardesty could almost feel.

Hardesty took another step back and looked at Johnny, shaking his head. "You're more growed than I thought," he said.

"His name," Johnny said again.

"They call him Cutter. I don't know what his real name is."

Johnny unclenched his fists and drew in a deep breath. He let it out slow, then drew another, even deeper breath.

"I know who he is," Johnny said. "I know his real name. I heard if often enough from Papa."

"He comes from down south someplace is all I know," Hardesty said.

Johnny's face turned rigid, frozen in a cold anger that flowed from his heart. His father had told him all about Cutter and his reputation. For his father's and Cutter's paths had crossed before, long before they had come to Sibley less than a half-dozen years before.

"His real name is Frank Sturgeon," Johnny said. "His pa was a white man, but his ma was a full-blood Cherokee. Papa said he was called Surgeon for a time, because of his liking for the knife and his habit of cutting on people he didn't like."

"How come you know all this, Johnny?" Hardesty asked.

"Pa told me about him when I was a kid. He shoed a horse for him and saw him cut a man up in St. Louis when we come through there."

"I heard he was real bad."

"I guess they started calling him Cutter a few years ago and the name just stuck. Do you know what he looks like now?"

"Yeah. I seen him real good. He's a swarthy, dark-complexioned man, with straight black hair that comes down to his shoulders. He's got eyes brown as roasted coffee beans, but one of 'em's a milk-eye."

"Yes, Papa told me he's got a speck of white in it. Right eye, I think."

"Yes, his right eye. When he looks straight at you, it'll pure freeze your blood."

"I wondered about all that blood on my papa's back when I held him in my arms," Johnny said. "And now I know. Cutter knifed him in the back, the bastard."

"Yeah, and he lit a shuck, like I said."

"Any idea where he might have gone, Phill?"

"Well, the other Maggard brothers went trapping up the Missouri last winter. They ought to be coming back right soon. Maybe Cutter went to tell them about Nate."

Johnny drew in a breath through his nostrils as if to feed oxygen to his thoughts. He knew the Maggard brothers were trappers. They had gone up the Missouri late last summer, along with several others in a loose-knit brigade. He remembered wishing that he had gone with them. He had wanted to, but his father had held him back with a warning. "You finish your schoolin', Johnny," he had said. "Them trappers are a bunch of wild men. They get out in the wilderness and they're nothin' but animals. That's no life for you."

But Johnny had nurtured a longing for the free wild life of the fur trappers ever since they had come to Sibley—even as far back as St. Louis, when he had seen young men arrive by foot or by boat and set off for the western mountains with nothing but a rifle, pistol, hatchet, and traps. He had dreamed of embarking on such a life since he was ten years old.

"I think you're right. Cutter has probably gone up the Missouri," Johnny said. "To tell them about Nate, I'm sure."

"Somebody's sure as hell gone to tell them, you can bet on that," Hardesty said.

"Then I've made up my mind," Johnny said. "I'm going

after Cutter. He's the one who's got to pay for killing my papa."

"He'll be far west of here," Hardesty said. "He's been there before and I heard tell he's more Injun than white, so you likely won't find him right off. But I'm glad you're goin'."

"Why?"

"I buried your ma a year ago, and now I got to bury poor Bill. I don't fancy havin' to dig your grave, too."

"Any graves get dug, I'll dig 'em from now on."

"You sound like you've growed up already, son."

"Maybe I have, Phill," Johnny said. "There's no one left but me with Papa and Mama gone. And Cutter's got to pay for what he done."

"When will you be goin' then?" Hardesty asked.

"I'll be saying good-bye to my papa right quick, and by sunup, I'll be riding out after Cutter. I shouldn't have any trouble finding his trail."

"You be careful, son. Cutter may want you to find him."

"What's that mean?"

"If he figures you'll be after him, he might make it easy for you. You're liable to ride around a bend in the trail and find him waiting for you, his rifle cocked to shoot you down."

"I'll have to watch it then, won't I, Phill?"

"If you get past Cutter, you still got the Maggard brothers to worry about. No tellin' where they be right now, but you can bet they'll shadder you to the ends of the earth huntin' you down. Nate was a twin, you know."

"No, I didn't. Does that make a difference?"

"The brothers doted on them twins, 'specially the youngest, Elijah."

"Isn't Cletus the oldest?" Johnny asked.

"Yep, and Nate's twin is Jedediah."

"How come Nate didn't ride west with his brothers?"

" 'Cause he didn't like work that much."

They both heard the front door creak. Johnny turned his head and saw Paddy framed in the dim light of the open doorway.

"Johnny, you can come in now if you like," Paddy said.

"Best go on and say your good-byes," Hardesty said.

"You coming in?"

"Yeah, I reckon."

The two men walked back to the porch and went inside. Mrs. Coombs had laid out Johnny's father on the big table in her dining room. He was dressed in the clothes and shoes Johnny had brought over. His skin looked darker than it had when he was alive. She had put something, powder, Johnny thought, and maybe some cream on the facial cuts, and his hair was combed over his head wounds.

"He looks right nice, Mrs. Coombs," Johnny said.

Lucy Coombs smiled wanly.

"Johnny," Paddy said. "I looked at that knife wound in your pa's back. The blade went in quick and deep. Bill didn't suffer much."

"Thanks, Paddy. I've got some favors to ask of you."

"Oh, and what might they be, Johnny-boy?"

"I'm going to take Blue and go after Cutter, and I was wondering if you might take care of Papa's horse."

"I can tend to him. When are you leaving?"

"As soon as I can get my things together for the trip. Hopefully, I'll be gone before the sun comes up."

"Too bad ye can't wait a day or two," Paddy said. "I really wanted you to meet my family. 'Specially my beautiful niece, Caitlin."

"Can't be helped, Paddy. I don't want Cutter's trail to go cold."

"I understand, my Johnny, but you don't know what you're missin'. If you was to lay your eyes on Caitlin, you might not want to ride off at all."

"Don't tempt me. If you want to stay in our house, you'd be welcome." Johnny knew that Paddy lived in squalor, a small hut that was no more than a shack.

"I'd take care of your house, too," Paddy said.

"And one more thing."

"Yes?"

"You've always been a big help around the shop and I know Papa thought highly of you. Do you think you could do some blacksmithing there?"

Paddy beamed then. "Me, a blacksmith? Well, I've watched your pa enough. I think I could do it. Not as well as he, of course. You plan to come back then?"

"I don't know. But I just hate to ride off and leave everything empty and untended. I'd be mighty grateful if you could live in the house and tend to the smithing."

"Why, I'd be proud, son. Mighty proud."

"We'll take care of things while you're gone, Johnny," Phill said. "You just take care of yourself. And come back."

"I'll do my best," Johnny said.

"Let's leave the boy alone," Mrs. Coombs said. "That coffee I made ought to be boiled by now. Paddy, you and Phill come on out to the kitchen."

The two men left with Mrs. Coombs, and Johnny was alone with the body of his father. There were two lamps burning, and they cast a coppery glow over the corpse on the table.

"Pa, I—I'm real sorry," Johnny said, fighting back tears. "I wish I could have been there to help you. I won't let Cutter get away with it."

Then Johnny fell silent. He closed his eyes and tried to pray, but he couldn't think of any words. He could only think of Cutter and what he had done to his father. It was hard to believe that his father was dead, that the man on the table had once been alive, breathing and talking and laughing.

"Damn you, Cutter," Johnny said, and then he turned away, no longer able to look at his father's hideous remains. He touched his father's hand, and it was cold and stiff. He squeezed it anyway in a final farewell.

"I hope you go to Heaven, Papa," Johnny said, his voice choked with emotion.

And then he broke down and cried, and he didn't care who heard him.

He stumbled out of the house, still sobbing, and he didn't say good-bye.

7

JOHNNY PACKED UP THAT NIGHT AND SADDLED HIS horse, Blue. He carried his father's Kentucky rifle, three pistols, and plenty of powder and ball and foodstuffs and cooking utensils to last him a good long time. He had learned to track from his father when they journeyed west, and he hadn't forgotten any of the lessons he'd learned.

And from traveling overland, he knew how to take care of his horse and live off the land. There was an abundance of game on the plain, he knew, and he planned to make meat to sustain himself. But he had coffee, flour, sugar, and beans and he knew how to cook. He had also packed some jerky, salt, pepper, lard, dried vegetables, and some dried apricots. He expected to pick up Cutter's tracks that same night or early in the morning, but he didn't want the killer to get too far ahead of him.

As he rode out of town, with the moon sailing high above him, Johnny scanned the ground for the track he sought. It would be a single track, one horse, and it could be most anywhere. But if his hunch was right, Cutter would not head east. He would go south, north, or west, and it was likely he'd head west to join up with the Maggard brothers. There was safety in numbers.

But Johnny vowed that if he did not find a single track going west, he would make a wide circle just to be sure. His eyes were keen and he knew what to look for. At that time of night, there would not be people leaving Fort Osage or Sibley. There would only be a lone man on the run, a killer.

Johnny thought it most likely that Cutter would head north, to Omaha, and he set out in that direction. His stomach roiled with an emptiness that gnawed at his innards. He suddenly realized that he hadn't eaten all day. He fished around in his saddlebag for some of the food-stuffs he had brought, and found the beef jerky he had packed in a thin wet towel. He chewed on a flattened piece of dried meat, and washed the food down with water from one of the three wooden canteens he had brought, having filled them just before he left home.

He found the tracks he was looking for shortly after leaving Sibley, a single set of horse tracks heading north. In the darkness he could not make out anything distinctive about the tracks, but he knew he would see more when the daylight came. For now, he was content that he was following Cutter, and that was all that mattered. He kept the tracks in sight, just in case Cutter tried to double back or leave the road in order to throw off any pursuers. From the stride of the horse, Johnny determined that he had been in no hurry, that he was probably pretty sure of himself.

Not far from town, perhaps an hour's ride, something on the side of the road caught Johnny's eye. Moonlight glinted on an object that shouldn't have been there. It was not part of the natural setting.

Johnny rode over to the object and looked down at it. He couldn't make out what it was, but he knew it wasn't natural. He spoke to Blue and swung out of the saddle. He bent down and studied the object, then picked it up gingerly by its lid.

"You sonofabitch," Johnny breathed. "You couldn't wait, could you?"

Johnny turned the object around just to make sure. He shook it and listened to its vacant rattle. He had found his father's strongbox. There was no mistaking that. And it was empty, cracked open like an eggshell, all of the money and coins gone.

Johnny tossed the box aside and remounted Blue, the anger in him like a smoldering fire. Cutter must be feeling pretty smug by now, he thought. He had the money he had stolen and he had gotten away clean. Or so he probably thought.

Now Johnny was even more alert than before, even though he was lacking in sleep. He thought Cutter might run to ground, make camp somewhere once he was well away from the fort and the settlement, and Johnny didn't want to stumble over him in the dark. His veins tingled with excitement. Although Cutter had several hours head start, finding the strongbox had brought the killer close to Johnny. He knew he was on his trail.

Johnny made a decision then. Eating had made him sleepy, and he knew he could be riding into danger if he kept on through the night. But if he stopped to sleep, he might also be vulnerable to someone sneaking up on him. But if he was going to sleep, he knew he was safer finding a place well off the road in the vicinity of where Cutter had left the broken strongbox. This seemed the most logical thing to do just then. So he left the road and rode some distance away looking for a spot where he might find concealment. The ground was uneven and broken by hillocks and shallow gullies, and there were trees growing here and there.

He was careful to keep his bearings as he searched for the perfect spot to make a dry camp for the night. Finally he saw what he was looking for, a depression large enough for him and his horse, a shallow place that was still deep enough so that, once down inside it, neither he nor Blue could be seen from the road.

Johnny rode behind the slight rise and into the washout. He dismounted and hobbled his horse. Then he walked out and onto the other side of the hillock for a ways. From there, he could not see the place he had chosen. He returned, unsaddled Blue, and laid out his bedroll. He made sure he had his rifle and pistols next to him when he lay down to sleep. He suddenly realized how tired he was when he began to relax. The strain of the day had begun to tell on him long before he had decided to rest, and now, alone, he felt the full weight of all that had happened; his father's murder being the most paramount in his mind.

Johnny closed his eyes and let sleep overtake him as he stared up at the stars and the broad band of lights that was the Milky Way. He found the Big Dipper, and Polaris, the North Star. He stared at them as his eyelids grew heavy, and when he finally closed his eyes, he blotted out all light and descended into the darkness of a heavy sleep.

Johnny slept fitfully, with dreams of food and bad men all mixed up. In his dream, he went to a place with large rooms and tables heaped high with delicious victuals that he could never quite reach. There was always a man there to block his way, and the man carried a knife that writhed in his hand like a silver snake. Then Johnny would climb stairs and go down dark passageways into other rooms that had tables set up for dining and steaming bowls and plates of venison, rabbits, quail, and dove, potatoes and biscuits and beans. His stomach grew teeth that gnawed at his belly, and men with guns would chase after him and his own pistols would not work. He could not load powder and ball into them because the barrels were not bored, and when he did find a pistol that was loaded, the flint wouldn't spark or the lock was attached backward so that the sparks flew at his face.

He awoke with a raging hunger sometime before dawn. When he first opened his eyes, he thought he was back home in his own bed, but gradually, as he stared at the sky filled with paling stars, he remembered where he was. Something was digging into his side, into his back. He reached down and felt the butt of his father's pistol. It had worked its way underneath him.

It was cold, and Johnny wanted to light a fire after he arose from his bedroll, but he knew he dared not risk it. The first thing he did was look for Blue, and when he didn't see him anywhere, a feeling of panic arose in him, an explosion of raw fear in his brain. Quickly he ran to the end of the shallow gully and walked to the top. There, a few yards away, Blue was grazing, his hobbles still intact. The horse whickered when Johnny walked up to him.

"You gave me quite a fright, Blue," Johnny said, rubbing the horse behind its ears. "If you keep this up, I'm going to have to rope you down."

The horse whickered again, and Johnny grabbed the short halter rope and led him back down into the hollow of the earth where he had spent the night.

Johnny gave Blue only a handful of grain that morning, since they had not traveled that far. He ate quickly while he was saddling up, chewing on hardtack and jerky. He missed not having any coffee, but he wanted to get a good start on the day. He hoped Cutter had holed up somewhere during the night. He would know later on by the freshness of the killer's tracks as he followed them northward.

Johnny was back on the road just before the sun rose over the eastern horizon, lighting the land with a brisk suddenness that took his breath away. Cutter's tracks stood out plain, and he halted to look at them more closely, fix them in his mind.

Johnny dismounted, then hunkered down to study all four hoofprints of the horse Cutter was riding. He knew right away that his father had not shod Cutter's horse. One shoe, the right rear, was oversized and the horse occasionally dragged it, leaving a scuff mark in the dirt. Another, the left front, had a nick in it, and when the horse was walking, it left a distinct mark in the ground.

Another shoe seemed to be on crooked, only slightly, but it might have been only that the horse was favoring that right rear hoof, since the canted one was the left rear. The right front shoe was worn on one side, and should have been changed some time ago.

Johnny walked along, leading Blue, studying the tracks, while some memory ticked away in his mind. He knew he had seen these tracks before, but where? And when?

It was a habit Johnny had picked up from his father, who had always looked at horse tracks with an eye toward drumming up business for his blacksmith shop. His father could tell by a horse's tracks when it might need a shoeing, and he'd shown Johnny the telltale signs of a worn or loose shoe.

But the answer would not come just then. Johnny just knew he had seen tracks like these somewhere before and had probably made a mental note of them without thinking. Perhaps, he thought, he had just seen the tracks in town, and had not put them with a particular horse as he usually did. In his mind, though, he could see his father checking tracks in town and following them to the horse that made them, then checking the shoes and finding the owner to tell him his mount needed shoeing.

Johnny finished looking at the tracks and climbed back on Blue and rode on, mulling over what he had learned. The tracks he was following this morning were already starting to fade. He had looked very closely at them, getting down to eye level so that he could detect the way the sides of the impressions had begun to crumble. He had seen the morning dew on them, which would soon dissipate as the sun rose in the morning sky.

So now he knew that the tracks had been made the

night before. Later, he would climb down from his horse and look closely at the tracks again and put an age to them. He hoped he could tell from horseback when the tracks began to look fresher. These tracks, he figured, were more than eight hours old, probably made closer to ten or twelve hours ago.

The tracks were deep-sunk, so Johnny knew the horse was packing a load. And he knew that Cutter was a big man, like his father, Jesse Sturgeon, who had died a couple of years ago in Sibley, where he had been living with the Maggard family. He had seen Jesse more than once, and his wife, too, the Indian woman. She had gone back to her people after Jesse died. Cutter had never come to bury his father either, which Johnny had thought curious until he learned that Cutter had hated both his father and mother, although no one knew why.

One thing, though. Cutter and the Maggards were friends, which was why Jesse had gone to live with them. Johnny thought maybe they were kin, cousins maybe. He knew now that Cutter and Nate had been friends, had both schemed to murder his father and steal his money.

And he knew that the Maggard brothers would shake out their ropes and come after him once Cutter told them Bill Stagg's boy had killed Nate. That was certain sure, Johnny knew.

He rode at a good pace, following Cutter's trail, and he was not surprised that Cutter had forded the Missouri and was now following the Kansas River, heading west. Johnny stopped every so often to study the tracks, and he saw that he was gaining little pieces of time. He knew where Cutter stopped to roll a smoke and relieve himself, and he knew where Cutter had stopped to let his horse drink and to fill his own canteen.

And by the end of the day, he knew that Cutter was following the wagon tracks of emigrants that had left deep ruts in the trail. Old tracks, probably from last summer, Johnny reasoned.

By the time the sun was setting, Johnny was aching in every bone, but he knew he was gaining on Cutter. And the country was opening up to him, and coming into him with all its grandeur and beauty. Blue was holding up well, not tiring, yet holding to a hard gait that ate up the miles. But just before he made camp that night, Johnny was dismayed to lose Cutter's tracks. Even the wagon ruts had disappeared, and Cutter's tracks became lost in a maze of those made by animals he had never seen before, but had only heard about.

Johnny had ridden into a maze of tracks that made him gasp in awe. These had obliterated Cutter's tracks less than an hour before he had come upon them. And they were made by a huge herd of buffalo.

8

JOHNNY FELT STRANGE AS HE FOLLOWED THE TRACKS
Cutter had left in his flight. At times, everything that had
happened, everything that he had left behind, seemed un-
real. It was as if he had entered another world, an alien
world where he was the only inhabitant. He realized as
he rode that he was all alone, but he also realized that this
was dangerous thinking.

He was alone, of course, but the tracks he was following were real, and the man he was hunting was also real.
It was just that he could see Cutter only in his mind, and
that picture was not always clear. He was beginning to
form a different picture of the man just by looking at the
tracks of his horse and studying when and where Cutter
stopped. At those times, he wondered what a man like
that could be thinking. Was he aware that someone was
following him? Or did he think he had gotten away clean?
From the tracks and his behavior, Johnny could not tell,
could not say for certain what a killer like Cutter was
thinking or feeling.

But in his solitary trek, Johnny's mind was full of speculation. There were times when he imagined that he was
Ulysses, sailing over the seas, wandering where the winds

blew him and fighting unknown forces at every turn, cursing the gods who had dealt him such a fate.

Johnny was glad he had brought the loose pages of Homer's book with him. He had left the heavy cover behind, but had, at the last minute, decided to bring what was left of the book with him. He had wrapped the pages in a pair of duck trousers and wrapped those with his slicker to keep the pages dry. As he thought about having the book with him, he did not feel so alone. When he read books, he felt a kinship with the writer and was able to live the life of the hero in his mind. He was doing that now as he rode through what seemed like an endless sea of high grass surrounding him on the road.

Once in a while, he would see a place where wagons had pulled through the grass and trampled it down, cleared a spot for people to spend the night or rest in a treeless spot before moving on. Those places, too, gave him comfort, because they showed signs of people having been there before him. And they, too, had gazed at the huge blue bowl of the sky and gazed at the vast expanse of desolate landscape that seemed endless as a man rode from sun to sun.

At the end of his second day of tracking, Johnny took a long time to study Cutter's tracks before laying out his bedroll in a place near the river, but well off the road. He took care in going into the high grasses, and then closed the path behind him by raising the grasses Blue had trampled. Then he had walked his horse to still another spot where he was concealed to some degree from the road, yet was near the river.

By his reckoning, Johnny had only gained an hour or two in pursuit of Cutter. Cutter did not stop much, and he kept a steady pace. But Johnny was gradually gaining on his quarry, and that gave him some comfort.

He thought that evening that Cutter was still far enough in front of him that it might be safe to build a small fire.

He had seen dried driftwood along the bank of the Kansas, and after he had made his choice to bed down for the night, he began to gather firewood, always walking through the grasses along different paths so that he would not leave a direct trail to where he would be sleeping.

Doing these things gave Johnny renewed energy after a long tiring day in the saddle. His legs ached, but less so than they did on that first night, and his butt was not so tender as it had been. It had been a long time since he had ridden so far on a horse, and he had discovered muscles he didn't know he'd had, in his calves, in his back, in his legs and thighs.

Johnny lit his fire before the sun set, and made sure to fan the smoke away so that it did not leave a telltale column in the sky. He filled his canteens and his coffeepot, set out his cooking utensils. He read some from Homer as the fire descended from flames to bright warm coals that gave off some light, but was not visible above the grasses. He put more of the mixed-up pages in order, cleaned dirt and offal from others, smoothed out those that were crumpled. He did this while trying to quell the anger he felt at the boys who had desecrated such a book. At the same time he felt superior to them, for they had not realized what a treasure they were fouling when they trampled and tore up Homer's brilliant pages.

Johnny walked along the riverbank with his father's rifle. He had loaded it with only forty grains of powder, and when he saw the jackrabbit freeze, he put the rifle to his shoulder. He lined up the blade front sight with the rear buckhorn to a point right behind the rabbit's left front leg. He squeezed the trigger and the rifle barked, belched out flame and white smoke. When he walked through the wisps of smoke, he saw that the rabbit was down, dead, with only his hind feet twitching in a final muscle spasm. Johnny smiled. The rifle had felt good when he fired it and the good shot had given him confidence. He held up

the rabbit, as proud as he had been when he shot his first
rabbit when he was only twelve.

Before fixing his supper, Johnny gave Blue a good rub-
down with wads of grass, checked his legs, ankles, fet-
locks, and shoes. Then he grained him, feeding him two
generous handfuls after he hobbled him so that he would
not stray.

Johnny cooked a small cake of bannock while the coffee boiled, just so he could taste something different than
the beef jerky he'd been munching on for two days. He
downed two dried apricots when he finished eating, chewing them well to extract all the flavor and remoisten them.
He ate the last piece of bannock with his last cup of coffee, then kicked dirt on the fire until it was fully smothered. He would not have coffee in the morning, he knew.
He wanted to ride away before the sun was up, and he
didn't want to have to light another fire.

He sat for a while in the dark and looked up at the
night sky, marking the constellations that he knew, taking
his bearings from the North Star in the Little Dipper.

Sometime during the night he was awakened by what
he thought was distant thunder. But when he looked heav-
enward, the stars were still clear and the moon was sailing
cloudless overhead like a bright shining eye. Puzzled,
Johnny went back to sleep and dreamed of his father and
mother. In the dream, they were still alive.

He woke up well before dawn, thinking about the Maggard brothers. He realized he didn't know much about
them. He knew they had lived wild lives, hunting and
trapping out in the western wilderness. When the fur mar-
ket collapsed, they had continued to live the same way,
hunting, trapping, skinning animals. He had heard they
were all dishonest, but nobody had ever had anything spe-
cific to say about that particular trait. He had seen them
return to Sibley every summer, never early in the spring.
They always spent their time there drinking and gambling

in the tavern, and then, along about August, they would leave again. Sometimes, he knew, they guided wagon trains going to Oregon or California, but only if it suited them.

As for Cutter, he knew even less about him, about how he lived, where he spent his time. But Johnny knew that Cutter and the Maggards were good friends and there were stories about them robbing pilgrims, and even hints that they sometimes killed innocent people who had come through town and were never seen again. From time to time, a relative would come through from back East and inquire about someone who had hired the Maggards to take them out West.

Now Johnny wished he had paid more attention to all the stories. But gossip was cheap in a town like Sibley, and there were stories to go with most everyone who had ever lived there, or passed on through.

There was still some rabbit left from supper, and Johnny ate that while he rolled up his bed and saddled Blue. He gave his horse another handful of grain and watered him at the river. He filled the canteen he had drunk from overnight, packed all his gear in the saddlebags, and rode out of his night camp in the darkness, knowing he could find the road easily.

As the stars began to fade in the sky, he was again tracking Cutter. Blue was frisky and he had to hold him back. The horse was acting strangely, Johnny thought, sniffing the wind, spooking at every clump and shadow.

Cutter's tracks became more difficult to follow as they left the worn trail and headed into rough, untrammeled country. Johnny was puzzled, but he had no choice. Every time he thought about giving up and going back home, he thought of what Cutter had done to his father. His anger boiled up constantly and became the fuel that kept him going, until his eyes ached from the strain of looking at hoofprints and his body ached from the hard saddle, the relentless heat of the sun.

Evidently, he thought, Cutter knew where he was going, so either he must be meeting someone, or he had a hideout where he would feel safe.

The land became more rugged and, more than once, the tracks skirted deep gullies, washouts from sudden floods, earth eroded at every turn. Johnny kept looking for some high point of land where Cutter might be able to view his backtrail, but he had seen no such landmark. Nor did he discern that Cutter was deliberately trying to throw anyone following him off track. The hoofprints seemed to go in straight lines until they veered off slightly as the rider changed course.

"Where in hell is Cutter going?" Johnny asked out loud late that afternoon.

For all he could see was empty land, with no signs of habitation, no sign of anyone having ridden this way ever before. But late in the afternoon, he rode out of the grass and onto a great flat place where nothing seemed to grow. The ground was torn up, too, roiled with the tracks of various animals. And as he rode, his horse kicked up dust.

The bare place cut a wide swath through the grass and resembled some ancient thoroughfare that had been abandoned. The maze of tracks gave him little information, but Blue became very nervous as they rode across it, following Cutter's tracks. Those tracks stood out because they were on top of all the others.

Late in the afternoon, Johnny reached the grassy plain again and the tracking became even more difficult.

But as the sun fell away in the western sky, he saw a pattern that helped him track Cutter. Cutter was riding on a parallel course to the barren swatch in the land, heading west and northerly.

Still, Johnny felt something else as he followed this new trail. Cutter was up to something, and he began to feel as if he was being watched. Blue's nervousness became more pronounced, and there were times when Blue balked and tried to turn back.

Once, as the sun was setting, Johnny heard that same sound he had heard during the night. It sounded like thunder, but when he again looked at the sky, he saw only puffs of white clouds and blue sky in every direction.

Blue came to a sudden halt, and Johnny listened. The sound was far away, but it sounded ominous to him. Blue's ears twitched and stiffened to cones that twisted in a half circle as the horse stood stiff-legged.

"What is it, boy?" Johnny asked, knowing there would be no answer.

But he listened as intently as Blue, and it seemed that the wind died away and left only a great silence.

9

THE SILENCE DID NOT LAST LONG.

Johnny heard the thunder again, and knew that he had misjudged the age of the buffalo tracks in his first hasty look. They had caught him by surprise and, so intent had he been to find Cutter's tracks among the mass of buffalo hoofprints, he had thought they must have come by long before.

Johnny rode on up the rise in the direction of the noise. As he topped the rise, he saw them, thousands of them, blanketing the land in all directions, roaming back and forth across the plains in small bunches as if lost. But then he saw others lining the river to drink, and then still others grazing while great swarms of them pounded the earth so that it shook beneath his horse's feet.

It was an awesome sight that took Johnny's breath away, and he felt Blue quivering under the saddle, his ears twitching, hardened to cones that twisted all around to pick up every rumble, every snort.

"Easy, boy," Johnny said as he patted Blue's neck to calm him.

Johnny sat there in the saddle, transfixed by the grand spectacle of the immense herd of buffalo. He saw now that the herd was getting larger as animals streamed in from the north and south, swelling the herd, as if called to this grand meeting on the wide prairie. As he watched, the noise grew louder until the sound was one long continuous roll of thunder that stirred his senses to a high-pitched tingling that he could feel with his entire body. When the noise became deafening, Johnny turned and saw that he and Blue were about to be overrun by still another enormous herd streaming in from the southeast. Behind it, the sky was blotted out with a huge cloud of dust that rose to the sky.

"Come on, boy," Johnny said, "let's get the hell out of here."

Johnny touched spurs to Blue's flanks and headed in the only direction that seemed safe, through a gap in the herd that led to the north. Soon, he was riding close to galloping shaggy beasts on either side of him, his own heart lodged in his throat, his ears pounding almost to deafness, his senses clanging like alarm bells.

Blue dodged a charging bull as Johnny held his breath and felt the clammy clutch of fear paralyze his throat. He spat out dust as he rode through the smothering cloud thrown up by thousands of hooves, riding blindly into still more dust and passing close to more buffalo all charging at full speed to some unknown destination.

For two days, Johnny rode around the herd, half-asleep in his saddle, his throat parched from the sun and the dust, his face and arms caked with sweat and clinging earth, his senses jangled to a terror-stricken morass.

Blue was exhausted and could no longer run. The horse just picked its way through the small herds that threatened to trample them at every turn, and Johnny hung onto the saddlehorn, afraid he might fall off and be ground to powder under the slashing hooves of mindless beasts romping at full speed like a single body, all packed together, all

streaming toward the main herd as if called there by some
ancient instinct that he could not fathom.

Johnny swung wide of the herd and rode a long circle
hoping to avoid being knocked down and ground underfoot. The dust was thick, and for a time, he could not see
how large the herd was, could only see flashes of hide
and horns. But as he rounded an empty place where the
buffalo had been, but were no longer, the wind came up
and started blowing the dust in the wake of the stampede.
The dust swirled and rose into the air, and he saw the
rumps of the buffalo as they headed away from him.
Johnny let out a sigh of relief.

It was then that he saw the riders, saw flashes of orange
flame, and seconds later, heard the crack of rifles. He
reined up Blue to take a better look. The riders were flank-
ing the rear of the herd, riding back and forth, reloading
from the saddle. He marveled at this feat for he knew how
difficult it was to load a flintlock not only on horseback,
but even while moving on foot.

He noticed also that the men were timing their shots
and their reloading, keeping pressure on the herd. When
one would fire, another would wait until that man began
to reload, then charge in close and fire. By the time the
first man was reloaded and ready to fire, the third man
was taking aim and squeezing the trigger.

Above the din of the thundering herd and the rifle fire,
Johnny heard another sound, and turned to see what was
making the noise.

Wagons were streaming into the dust and stopping.
Men disembarked and ran to the slain buffalo. Some had
pistols, while others had rifles. If any buffalo was alive,
these men dispatched them with a shot to the back of the
head, severing the spine. Then these men drew long shining knives and began to cut up the buffalo. Johnny saw
that they were skinning them, not to take the meat, but
only the hides. He counted six wagons and a dozen men,

at least. He had never seen anything like it in his life and he sat there, dumbstruck at the efficiency of the hiders and the numbers of buffalo downed by the three horsemen.

Sensing trouble, Johnny widened his circle, but kept his eye on the skinners taking off the buffalo hides and loading them in the wagons. Soon he no longer heard the thunder of thousands of buffalo hooves and he no longer heard the crack of rifles.

Finally, as he was rounding the last part of the circle on untrammeled ground, he saw the three riders coming back to join the men with the wagons. They were laughing and talking loudly. They seemed happy at the work they had done.

Johnny dismounted in the tall grass so that he would not be seen should any man look his way. From where he stood, he could see the three riders plainly as they drew closer to the wagons. He could hear snatches of conversation that made no sense, for the wind was still blowing away from him and toward the hiders and the hunters.

Johnny, on a hunch, ground-tied Blue to a thick bunch of grasses he twisted together. He took his rifle from its scabbard and started sneaking toward the nearest wagon. He hunched over so that his head was below the tall grass. Every so often, he stopped and took a look.

The last time he stopped to peer at the men, the riders had reached one of the wagons, but still sat their horses.

He could hear their voices better at that distance, and he could also see the faces of the hunters and what they were wearing. He froze as if his blood had suddenly turned chill.

Less than two hundred yards away, Johnny saw Nate Maggard's three brothers: Cletus, the eldest, his face bearded like his brothers'; Elijah, the youngest brother; and Nate's twin, Jedediah. He studied Jedediah's face, and had the eerie feeling that he was staring at Nate. The resemblance, even with the beard, was uncanny. Johnny shivered as gooseflesh appeared on his arms and the hairs on the back of his neck stood rigid, prickling like stinging nettles on his skin.

"Think, think," Johnny told himself as his pulse raced and his heartbeat throbbed in his right temple.

To calm himself, Johnny drew in a deep breath and held it while his mind cleared. Then he let it out again slowly and dropped to the ground. He hoped he was making the right decision as he began to crawl on hands and knees toward the wagon.

He could not see more than a foot or two, but he could hear. Something inside him told him to get closer so that he could listen to the conversation between the Maggards and the skinners. He moved inches at a time so that he would not reveal himself by the movement of the grasses he was burrowing through.

As he drew closer, moving like a prowling cat, he could make out more of the words. He stopped often to listen, ready to jump up and flee if his presence was discovered.

"Somebody's coming," one of the men said.

Johnny froze. His palms were slick with sweat. His heart suddenly started pounding at a rapid rate.

"I been expectin' this'n," Cletus Maggard said.

Johnny recognized his scratchy, deep voice. He wondered if they were talking about *him*.

"Yeah," Jedediah said.

"That your brother, Jed?" one of the skinners asked.

"Ha," Jedediah exclaimed. "More like the devil's brother."

Johnny heard laughter, then more talk that he couldn't hear. He crawled closer so that he could hear better, and he tried to slip through the grasses and not disturb them too much. His curiosity was greater than his fear just then. He knew now that someone else was being discussed, and that gave him some comfort. So far, he believed, he had not been spotted by either the Maggard brothers or the buffalo skinners.

"Ho," called out Cletus, and Johnny froze. It seemed to him that he was within a few feet of the men at the wagon, but he knew he couldn't be that close.

"Howdy, Clete," a man said, and Johnny knew it was the rider the Maggards had been talking about.

"You took your sweet time, Cutter," Cletus said. "Light down and we'll put on a pot for you."

Cutter. Johnny's heartbeat accelerated into a flutter of rapid thumps. Cutter. He had to see him, had to see that horse he rode, fix those images in his mind. He had to see the face of the murderer, the man who had killed his father.

Johnny saw something ahead of him that looked like perfect cover. At first he thought it was a mound of dirt, but as he crabbed toward it, he knew he had been mistaken. It was not a pile of dirt at all, not a mound in the middle of a grassy sea. None of those things.

It was a dead buffalo, a huge bull that lay still like some slain shaggy giant not far from where the skinners were butchering one of the animal's kin.

Johnny crawled in behind the buffalo and laid his rifle down while he wiped his clammy hands on the dead bull's hide to dry off the sweat.

He heard the sound of hoofbeats and then a silence as Cutter apparently rode up to the group by the wagon. He waited, listening.

"Where you bound, Cutter? Goin' to throw in with us, make yourself a few dollars?"

"Naw. I ain't luggin' one o' them heavy buffalo rifles around with me. I'll meet you at Bent's."

"Well, that's where we're goin'," Elijah said. "Next day or two, I reckon."

"Lije, you don't know beans about where we're goin' ner when," Cletus said.

Johnny summoned the courage to push himself up with both arms and peer over the hump of the dead buffalo. He was careful to move slowly and not make any noise. The first man he saw was Cutter, who was still on his horse. The others were all on foot.

Johnny looked at the horse, and knew that he had seen it before, in Sibley, but had not known it belonged to Cutter. The tracks he'd been following, he knew, belonged to that tall black horse with the blaze face and three white stockings.

The horse stood close to sixteen hands high, and it was packing two heavy saddlebags, two rifles slung on either side of the saddle, besides a bedroll and three canteens. Johnny counted at least three pistols hanging in holsters from the saddlehorn.

"Step down, Cutter," Cletus said. "You ain't in all that big a hurry."

"No, I ain't in no big hurry," Cutter said as he swung down from his saddle. " 'Sides, I brung you boys some pretty good gut-bustin' tanglefoot from Sibley to wet your whistles with."

Johnny watched as Cutter reached into one of his saddlebags and brought out a bottle of whiskey. He pulled the cork with his teeth and passed the bottle to Cletus, who swigged from it before handing it to Jedediah. The skinners stopped work, both of them, and walked over to join the growing circle of men.

"Tastes like Taos lightnin'," Jedediah said. "But it warms the cockles of my heart."

"Is that where your cockles is?" Cletus said.

"If you had any, you'd know where they is," Jedediah said.

" 'Fraid I got some bad news for you boys," Cutter said as the skinners both took swallows from the whiskey bottle.

"Bad news?" Jedediah asked. "It ain't about Nate, is it?"

"Yeah. I got bad news and more bad news."

"Spit it out then."

"You know Bill Stagg?"

"Yeah, we know him," Jedediah said. "That smithy there in Sibley."

"That's the one," Cutter said. "Well, him and your brother were playin' cards a coupla weeks ago and Nate caught Bill cheatin'. There was a fight and Nate put out Bill's lamp."

"Killed him?" Elijah asked.

"What do you think?" Jedediah said, a note of irritation in his voice.

"Glad Nate came out on top," Cletus said.

"Well, Bill's pup come in about then and didn't like it none that his pap was dead and he threw down on Nate. Shot him dead."

"Christ," Jedediah said.

"Oh, no," from Elijah.

"Damn." Cletus's eyes teared up and he bowed his head so that the others wouldn't see him cry.

"That little sonofabitch," Jedediah said. "I'll kill that bastard."

"Well, you may get your chance," Cutter said. "That's the more bad news I got to tell you."

"What do you mean?" Jedediah asked.

"That snot-nosed kid has been follerin' me like a shadder, doggin' my tracks like a stick-tight on my pants."

Johnny froze as the Maggard boys suddenly all started craning their necks in all directions as if hoping to spot him right out there in the open.

For a long minute, Johnny was sure that Jed Maggard was looking him straight in the eye. And he thought, God, don't let me die until I've killed that damned Cutter.

10

CUTTER SEEMED TO BE STARING RIGHT AT JOHNNY STAGG when he said something that made Johnny's muscles relax to a limpness that rendered him helpless for a moment.

"I think I lost the little bastard a day or two ago. But if I'm any judge, he'll run acrost my track sooner or later."

"Why in hell would Bill's kid come gunnin' for you, Cutter?" Jedediah asked.

Johnny's muscles returned to normal when Cutter just shrugged and said, "Beats the hell out of me."

"That don't make any sense, Cutter," Cletus said. "Has the boy gone plumb loco?"

"I dunno. Could be. It was a crazy thing he did, shootin' Nate."

"Well, I hope Johnny does show up," Jed said. "I'll tack his hair on my rifle stock, the sonofabitch."

"I can't believe Nate's dead," Elijah said, and Cletus started bawling out loud.

As Johnny stared, transfixed, Jed slapped Clete on the back and called to one of the skinners: "Let's have that whiskey bottle back over here, Dan."

Johnny had heard enough. He ducked his head behind

the dead buffalo hump and took in his first full breath since he had first laid eyes on Cutter. He looked at his rifle lying on the ground and mentally kicked himself for being so careless. He should have had it in his hand the whole time he was eavesdropping on the Maggards and Cutter.

Now he held the rifle close to his chest and slanted it so that the barrel would not stick up over the buffalo. He breathed slowly and deeply so that he would stop shaking. This was worse than buck fever, he thought. And it was far more dangerous. He knew that if Cutter and the Maggards discovered his presence, he would be shot dead.

"I still don't know why Bill's kid would be comin' after you, Cutter." Jedediah was persistent.

"Maybe he wants to kill the whole bunch of you, I don't know," Cutter said.

"Well, he's got him some balls if that's so."

"Nate was aimin' his pistol at young Johnny when the kid shot him. They was face-to-face."

"You don't say."

"It warn't no more'n a hair's difference. Course Nate wasn't expectin' the kid would really shoot, I reckon."

"Well, Nate made a big mistake," Jedediah said. "And so did Johnny Stagg."

"If I have anything to say about it," Cutter said, "it'd be Johnny's last mistake."

"I double that," Clete said.

"Me, too," Elijah piped in.

"Cutter, you want to stay for supper?" Jedediah asked. "Dan here's goin' to cook us up some buffler meat. And do you want the liver right now? Or the heart?"

Johnny's stomach turned when he heard Jed's invitation to Cutter.

"I reckon I could," Cutter replied. "Then I got to get to Bent's Fort. It's a long ride."

"We'll join you then, if you mean to stay around there at the Bent's."

"I'll be there a while."

Johnny had heard enough. He slid back down on his belly and started the slow crawl back to where he had left Blue. He didn't care to hear Cutter gulping down raw liver, or worse, a buffalo's heart.

It took Johnny most of the afternoon to reach his horse, and by the time he got to the place where he had left Blue, he was exhausted, both from the exertion and from the tension caused by fear and anxiety. His nerves jangled like a boxful of cowbells. He lay next to Blue for a long time, listening to every sound, just in case one of the skinners, Cutter, or the Maggards had found his tracks by the dead buffalo and were coming after him.

But nobody came after him that afternoon, and Johnny had time to think, to assess his situation. He led Blue well away from where he had seen the Maggards and Cutter, staying out of the saddle so that he would be harder to spot by a man on horseback riding in that place of gently rolling hills.

Doubts began to seep into Johnny's mind as he studied his situation. First of all, he had no idea where Bent's Fort was. He had heard some talk of it back in Sibley, had heard of the Bent brothers—William and, he thought, James. And their partner, someone named Ceran or St. Ceran, he wasn't sure. But where was it? On some river, he knew.

For now, he realized he was lost. He had no maps; he did not know the country. A feeling of overwhelming hopelessness descended on him as he realized he didn't even know the way back home, back to Sibley. In his blind rage to find and kill Cutter, he had paid little attention to where he was going and none at all to where he had been.

He could follow the stars, of course, and try to find his

way to the Missouri River, or the Kansas. But then what? His father's death would remain unavenged and he would be forced to live in fear for the rest of his life, waiting for the Maggard brothers to return to Sibley and kill him. There were three of them, and he knew he would stand little chance if they all came at him at once.

And then, what about Cutter? He would go unpunished for the murder of Johnny's father. And if the Maggards did come back to Sibley, Cutter would no doubt be with them, and then Johnny would be facing four men, instead of three.

As night fell, Johnny heard the rumble of wagons in the distance, and it somehow gave him a comforting feeling. The wagons meant people, and he had ridden for weeks with no one to talk to except his horse. He climbed back into the saddle as the sun was setting, and knew what he must do. He thought of his father then, but not with the homesickness that had gripped him all afternoon. He remembered a conversation they had had a few weeks after his mother had died.

Johnny and his father had sat outside their house at sunset one evening, watching the sky and the bull bats flying over the river, a river that was changing colors like some liquid painting, its waters filled with gold and silver and red and yellow and green.

"You know, Johnny, your mother's passing made me think of how it was when my own mother died. God, it seems like a hundred years ago now as I look back on it. But my papa took me aside for a talk one day after that and asked me what I would do if he was to die, too."

"That must have made you feel bad, Papa."

"At first, it hit me like a club and I got scared. I was about your age, I reckon, and I just couldn't think of what it would be like to be all alone in the world. An orphan."

"I know," Johnny had said. "I couldn't even think of you being gone now that Mama is passed."

"But you got to think of it, Johnny. It's going to happen one day."

"But not for a long time, Papa."

And even then, Johnny had felt the fear crawling up into his throat and his stomach fluttering as if it was filled with a cloud of winged insects. His mother's death had been bad enough, but to think of being left alone if his father died like that was just too horrible to think about.

"You aren't going to die for a long time, Papa."

"Who knows? We can't none of us say for certain when our time will come."

"Then let's not talk about it, Papa."

"I think it'll make more of an impression on you if we talk about this now, Johnny. While your mama's memory is still fresh in your mind. It's something you're going to have to face someday. Maybe not soon, but someday."

"Papa, I want you to grow to be real old. I'll take good care of you. By then, I'll be rich and married and have a bunch of kids who'll play at your feet."

His father had laughed and slapped him good-naturedly on the back.

"Well, I hope that's the way it happens, Johnny," his father had said. "But you mind my words. Death has a way of coming unexpectedly, without no warning. You just make sure you're man enough to bear up under it if something happens to me."

"We knew Mama was going to die," Johnny had said, his words coming out soft and feeble.

"We knew she was poorly, but we didn't know when she would die. I didn't think she'd die so soon, so young."

Johnny had heard the catch in his father's voice, and his own throat had squeezed up and throttled him just before he started bawling all over again. And his father had cried, too, that day, and they had talked no more about death from that moment on.

"I can carry the load, Papa," Johnny breathed as he

looked up at the darkening sky. Was his father up there in the sky? He did not know. That was something he and his father had never talked about after his mother died. And the only thing his father had said when they buried his mother was that "she's in Heaven."

Well, maybe that's where his papa was now, he thought. Maybe his mama and papa were together, looking down on him, knowing he was lonesome for them, knowing he was all alone and lost in the wilderness.

"No, I ain't, Blue," Johnny said in a louder voice this time. "I ain't lost. We can always find the river and we can follow it and it will take us back home."

But something began to squeeze his throat again, and he knew he was feeling sorry for himself and if he didn't look out, he would start crying, and that wouldn't be very manly and would only make things worse.

Especially, he thought, if his folks were up in Heaven looking down on him.

11

THE NIGHT BECAME JOHNNY'S HAVEN AND HARBOR AS
he rode back toward the place where he had overheard
Cutter and the Maggards talking. The night had sobered
him, calmed him, made him think hard about what he
must do.

He rode toward the dead buffalo he had hidden behind,
hoping the skinners had taken its hide and left the meat.
He was hungry, and there was enough meat in one carcass
to feed a family for a good long time. He had plans for
some of that meat, and his roiling stomach lent an urgency
to his mission.

He found the buffalo killed that afternoon, now skinned
so that it shone in the dark like some albino creature
hulked up on a seashore to rot in the next day's sun.
Johnny dismounted and tied his reins to one of the horns,
not the one jutted up like some giant's thumb, but to the
one beneath, which was dug into the ground from the
weight of the animal's fall.

Johnny knelt by the carcass and touched the meat,
pushing on it with his trembling fingers, following the
cuts the skinner had made to the huge cavity of its belly
and chest. He felt inside for the heart and liver, but they

had been taken. He put the blade of his knife to the beast's haunch and began sawing back and forth, putting pressure on the blade until he had started a bloodless line outlining a piece of meat that he could carve out as if he was a blind sculptor making a statue. He set the chunk on the ground, and began cutting off other chunks of meat that were easy to reach and did not take much effort. His heart was pounding the whole time because he felt like he was stealing from someone, and because he didn't know but that one of the Maggards or a skinner might come back to get some of the meat left behind.

But no one came, and Johnny knew he had cut more meat than he could carry or eat at one sitting, but he packed the chunks in his saddlebags, which had become somewhat leaner than when he had left Sibley, and he mounted Blue, who was somewhat spooky from being tied to the dead buffalo, and rode off into the night with purpose.

Finally, Johnny saw what he had been looking for, off in the distance, across the rolling landscape of the night, a small orange splash of light, and he knew it was the hunters' campfire and that was where the Maggards, Cutter, and the other skinners would be, taking their evening meal, talking among themselves by the fire.

Now that he knew where the Maggard camp was, Johnny rode in the opposite direction, but on a line that he could follow later to bring him near the night camp. He rode until he could no longer see the flame of the campfire, and rode still farther until he knew there was enough rolling earth between him and them. That was where he stopped to build a fire and cook some of the meat he had taken.

"Better'n beef meat," Johnny said to Blue when he had finished eating a portion of the buffalo meat. After supper, he cut the meat he had taken into smaller pieces, and some of these he carved into strips to dry in the sun while he was riding. He salted the rest down and wrapped each section in damp cloth, stored them loosely in his saddlebags.

Later, he heard the coyotes working the carcasses of the buffalo. Their cries carried on the night like a melodious chorus from some other world. He was sure they would remove all traces of his own work on one of the dead buffalo, but he didn't expect anyone to come back and check in the morning. Although he wouldn't put it past Cutter. From what he had heard, Cutter was pretty smart. He knew he had been followed from Sibley, and Johnny still wondered how he knew that he was on his trail. The man must have eyes in the back of his head, or else he had doubled back without being seen and known that Johnny was tracking him across the country.

Perhaps, Johnny thought, he should change his tactics. But how? He could not follow Cutter too closely, nor could he stay too far behind. If he didn't follow fresh tracks, there were too many chances that he would lose the murderer altogether. Cutter was smart enough to cover his trail, but there was also weather, the rain and the wind, that could obliterate tracks, age them so fast he would not be able to tell fresh from old.

Somehow, he knew, he had to find his way to Bent's Fort. That was where Cutter was going and that was where the Maggards would bring their buffalo hides to sell or trade.

And he had no idea where Bent's Fort was.

"But we'll get there, Blue, won't we?" Johnny said before he put out the fire and lay on his bedroll to look up at the stars and devise a plan for the morrow.

Blue snorted as if in reply, then continued to munch on grass. Hobbled as he was, the horse made little sound as he moved from clump to clump. But Johnny could hear him tearing the grasses loose and pulling them up into his mouth.

"Eat all you want, boy," Johnny said. "We may have us a long ride tomorrow."

Johnny fell asleep listening to the plaintive songs of the coyotes as they roamed the vast range of the night like packs of vagabonds, wandering minstrels coursing through the dark regions of dream.

Johnny awoke before dawn to a stillness that was like the quiet of graveyards, and yet his mind was ringing with the peals of coyote laughter from the night before, and these ribbons of choral melody sounded to him almost like the chants and keenings of the Osage back at the fort, as if the two sounds were one and the same and emanated from the same source through some alchemy of dream lingering like an unknown substance in his very blood. He shook from the chill and from the memories of those mornings at home that had somehow mingled with the ghostly images of the little gray dogs of the prairie howling him to sleep the night before.

"Blue?" Johnny said, as if needing the reassurance that the roan gelding was still there, and that Johnny was truly awake in his own world and not some wraith of a soul murdered in its sleep, turned to spirit and fed upon by little wolves.

Blue whickered at the sound of his name, and Johnny scanned the nightscape for his silhouette, sniffed for the scent of his sweated hide, some trace of the horse apples deposited in the grasses during the night.

Finally Johnny saw the dark mass shaped like a horse, shrunken by distance to pony size, and he breathed a sigh of relief. Blue stood, hobbled, some thirty or forty yards away, and the sky in the east was paling with a soft light that presaged the sun's bright rising, erasing those lights lowest in the sky.

He had dreamed, too, of that terrible moment when he had killed a man, Nate Maggard, and knew that he had not gotten over it, might never get over it. The memory of it still made him quiver inside, and sometimes it made his hands and legs shake. He had not wanted to kill anybody, and even though he knew he had taken a human life in self-defense, the deed had taken something out of him, ruined something of his that he could not name, be it his soul or his character or just his feelings. He wondered, if he had it to do all over again, if he could pull the trigger and make a man's life go away forever.

Johnny arose quickly, trying to shake off the bad thoughts that still lingered in his mind. Could vengeance, he wondered, wipe out the stain on his conscience as the light from the sun wiped out the stars? He did not know, and just then, he could not think about killing again, could not bring up his hatred of Cutter to put him in enough of a rage that he would go on and shoot the bastard down in cold blood to avenge the murder of his father.

He gave Blue some of the grain that was left and watered him before he tended to his own needs. As the land became brighter with the rising of the sun, he knew he was stalling, moving slowly and almost without purpose so that he would not have to go after Cutter again so soon.

He built a small fire, using dried grass and buffalo chips, and then put a pot on the fire to boil coffee. He put a strip of buffalo meat right on the fire and cooked it while the coffee water came to a boil. He chewed on the meat and drank his coffee, then put the fire out as the sun finally cleared the horizon. To the north, he saw clouds gathering, and wondered if there would be rain that day. He wondered, too, if Cutter was still with the Maggards, or if he had ridden off towards Bent's Fort. And if he had, where might Johnny pick up the tracks without running into the Maggards or any of the skinners.

Finally he saddled Blue and secured his bedroll in back of the cantle. He checked his flints and powder on the pistols and his rifle, cleaned his knife on the grasses, shook all of his canteens to see how much water he had left. Then he mounted up and rode that straight line he had memorized, back to the dead buffalo that had given him meat, and then rode the line from there to where he had seen the Maggards' campfire the night before.

To his surprise, the night camp was deserted and abandoned. He had expected he would have to skirt the encampment once he drew within sight of it. In fact, he had been prepared to put the spurs to Blue and ride for his life if anyone there had spotted him.

Johnny inspected the campground, saw the pile of bones thrown away the night before after the meat had been cooked and eaten. He saw where the skinners had drawn up their wagons in a circle around the camp and fire, and he saw the bedding places of the men, their boot prints, where they had relieved themselves at various times, and where they had put out their smokes.

Johnny stood up in the stirrups and scanned the land from horizon to horizon. He saw not a speck of dust nor any moving thing.

"They must have lit out mighty early, Blue," Johnny said, but even as he spoke those words, his skin began to prickle. Perhaps they had taken the wagons away and the Maggards had walked back with Cutter and hidden in the tall grass. Maybe, he thought, they were watching him.

He shook off that thought and began to look for Cutter's distinctive tracks, those left by his horse. In the maze of hoofprints and wagon tracks, he found Cutter's trail and began to follow it. For a long while, Cutter and the Maggards had ridden together, and then, the wagons had begun to veer off along the wide swath made by the buffalo herd.

So they were following the buffalo, Johnny thought. They would shoot more of them and skin them out until the wagons were loaded. How long would that take? Another day, two? A week? He did not know, and berated himself mentally for not counting the buffalo carcasses he had seen with his own eyes the day before. If they had luck, the Maggards would not take long to fill their wagons and head for Bent's Fort.

He was elated when, sometime later, he saw Cutter's horse tracks separate from those of the Maggard brothers.

"So, Cutter, you are going to Bent's Fort," he said aloud, and Blue snorted and tossed his head. "Well, so am I. So are we, Blue."

And Stagg rode on, following the path Cutter had taken, stopping every so often to stretch his legs and relieve himself. One of his canteens was empty. Another was about half full, and he still had one full canteen. He was counting on Cutter leading him to water, either that day or the next, so he was not yet worried about his supply. But he was concerned that he would not have enough water for himself and Blue if they did not cross a stream or come to a river sometime soon.

At least they were no longer following the buffalo, and he hoped that the Maggards would soon be far behind him.

Late in the afternoon, Johnny came to a small stream. It was marked by trees and bushes growing along its banks. He saw where Cutter had stopped to water his horse and fill his own canteens. The tracks were easy to read, and that made him slightly ill at ease. He had the sensation, while he was at the little creek, that Cutter was somewhere close by, watching him.

Stagg picked up Cutter's tracks on the other side of the creek, but this did not comfort him. The tracks were less than an hour old, and he knew that to follow Cutter so closely would be a big mistake that could cost him his life.

He marked the place where he left Cutter's trail and then doubled back to the creek. He rode along it for another hour, looking for a suitable place to camp for the night.

He was about to stop at a likely place when he heard noises that caught him by surprise. They seemed to be coming from just beyond a rise where the creek took a bend.

He heard voices and the creak of wagons, the snort of horses. He reined in Blue hard and sat there, listening. He pulled his rifle from its sheath and lay it across the pommel, every nerve in his body quivering like a plucked banjo string. He held his breath as he heard another sound close by.

Cutter?

The sound had turned him into a statue, and he was sure that his heart had stopped beating.

Johnny closed his eyes and waited for the shot that would kill him.

The sound he had heard was the metallic click of a rifle lock. Someone had cocked a gun and had him dead in his sights.

12

JOHNNY KNEW THE SOUND HE HAD HEARD HAD COME from behind him. He wondered if he could turn in time to shoot before a lead ball tore through his back. In that pause, a lifetime passed. In those fractions of seconds, he knew that Cutter had surely won, had outwitted him, outfoxed him, and would surely be pulling the trigger of his rifle before Johnny could take another breath.

Then *snick*. And Johnny felt as if his blood had turned to ice.

The man had a set trigger. Johnny had seen such rifles before. They had two triggers. One was used to set the other so that just a touch of pressure from the finger would set it off.

"Don't you even so much as twitch, pilgrim, or I'll blow a hole through you so big I could put my fist through it."

Stagg didn't recognize the voice, but the words made shivers splash up and down his spine.

"If you're going to shoot," Stagg said, "go ahead and do it. I don't fancy being tortured to death by your threatening tongue."

"Well, well, well. What have we got us here, a damned

brave man? Or a spineless coward who's plumb out of patience?"

"Neither one, mister. You got the drop on me. I know I can't beat that bullet in your barrel."

"You're damned right you can't, sonny boy. You're just a tick away from eternity. I touch this second trigger and you're wolf meat."

"I know," Stagg said.

He could not match the voice with a face. He wondered if it was Cutter who had the drop on him. If it was Cutter, the man might want to stick him with that Arkansas toothpick of his, just for pure meanness.

"You just hold real still, sonny, whilst I come around for a look-see at your face. I want to see for myself what a dumb pilgrim looks like."

Stagg didn't move, didn't twitch a muscle. He heard the man's footsteps as he circled around behind him. With every step, Johnny's fear grew like scratchy hair on his brain.

Finally the man stopped, but Johnny was looking straight ahead and couldn't see him out of the corner of his eye.

"So, you are just a whelp, ain't ye, sonny? Still wet behind the ears."

"I can't see what you look like," Stagg said.

"Well, I'm a sight prettier'n you are, I can tell you that, sonny boy. Just slide that rifle toward me, butt first. Easy now. Don't go makin' no sudden moves."

Johnny slid the rifle slowly to his right. Then suddenly, the man jerked it from his grasp.

"Well, now, this is a mighty fine Lancaster," the man said. "You don't see much curly maple beyond the Cumberland Gap. Where'd you get it?"

"It belonged to my father," Johnny said.

"He dead?"

"Yes."

"Turn around, sonny. I want to look at you real good."

Johnny turned and looked at the man standing next to
his horse. The man was tall, and he wore buckskins, but
they were unlike any he had ever seen. Just below the
shoulders, wide bands of colored beads were sewn to the
leather, and there were similar bands on the sleeves. He
wore boot moccasins that were also beaded. He carried a
possibles pouch and two powder horns, one small for the
fine powder, the other larger for the rougher granulation.
The man also had two large canteens slung over his shoulders. His face was masked by a thick, brushy beard. Blue
eyes crackled on either side of a large straight nose.

"Well, you are a young pup, ain't ye?"

"I'm old enough," Johnny said.

"For what? To get yourself kilt?"

"I don't mean you no harm, mister."

The man laughed, and Johnny felt anger building in
him as hot blood flooded the veins in his cheeks.

"I ain't much worried about you causin' me any harm,
youngster. Now, light down real slow and don't touch any
of them pistols you got on you."

Johnny grabbed the saddlehorn and swung off the left
side of the horse. The man in the buckskins had sidled
around so that he was now facing him. Johnny stood a
half foot taller than the man who held his rifle pointed at
him.

"You just walk on ahead of me with your horse, sonny.
Maybe you didn't mean any harm and maybe you did."

"Are you going to shoot me?" Johnny asked, but there
was no tremor in his voice. It was a flat, matter-of-fact
question.

"Ain't made my mind up yet. Just go on yonder over
that rise."

Johnny flicked the right rein over Blue's head and held
both reins in his hand as he started toward the source of
the noises he had heard earlier. He knew the man in buck-

skins was behind him, but he never heard any of his foot-steps, so soft were his moccasins touching the ground.

As he topped the rise, Johnny saw two wagons covered with a heavy tarp, eight mules standing in a rope corral next to the creek. There were four horses, all hobbled, grazing a few yards away from the center of camp. There was a big canvas lean-to pitched in one place, and two men gathering firewood while one was placing rocks in a circle in front of the lean-to. All of the men were wearing buckskins, and all of them had full beards. They all seemed to be in their thirties. The man behind him was older, perhaps forty or so.

"What you got there?" one of the men called out.

"He's got him a greenhorn kid," another said.

"Least it ain't no red nigger." The man placing the stones got up from his squat and grinned.

"Sonny, you just give me your horse and walk on in," Johnny's captor said. At the same time, the man pulled Johnny's pistol from its holster on his belt.

Johnny dropped the reins and walked close to the man at the stone fire ring, then stopped. He felt naked as the three men scoured him with their glances.

"You got a name?" The man closest to him was no longer grinning.

"I got one. Same as you."

"You got a right smart mouth, too, pilgrim."

Johnny said nothing.

"Go easy on him, boys. He ain't got much bark on him." This from the man who had Johnny's horse and who was tying Blue to a cottonwood sapling.

Johnny watched as the man who had brought him there removed the few strips of buffalo meat from atop Blue's saddlebags where Johnny had put them to dry. They had started to smell some, but he had hardly noticed it until now. The other two men walked over, and he thought they all smelled worse than the raw buffalo meat.

"Cat got your tongue?" one of the men asked.

"He's probably scairt," the other, who had come over, said.

"Naw, he jest ain't learnt to talk yet," said the man with a stick of dried wood still in his hand.

The man who had braced Johnny stepped up then and handed Johnny's rifle to the man nearest him. "Take a look at that, would you?" he said. Then he turned to Johnny and winked.

"These boys won't eat you, sonny. Let's hear your name. I know you can talk."

"J-Jo-Johnny Stagg. I mean, John Stagg."

"Well, which is it? They still call you Johnny, eh? Well, that's all right. You might grow out of it, if you live long enough."

Johnny felt the heat rising to his cheeks again. He began to think that these men weren't going to kill him, though. At first, when he was brought here at gunpoint, he hadn't been so sure.

"Set yourself down, young'un. I'm Lafon, Marshall Lafon, but you can call me Marsh."

"You a marshal?" Johnny asked.

All four men guffawed.

"That's his name," the fire-maker said. "I'm Calvin McTeague. Call me Cal."

"And I'm Frank Early." One of the other men stepped up and put out his hand. Johnny shook it.

"And I guess that leaves me," the last man said. "I'm Orville Baxter. They call me Orv."

"They call him Bastard sometimes, too," Lafon said. "Go ahead and set and let's hear all about you. Where do you hail from?"

"I come from Sibley."

"Sibley, eh. Fort Osage. Why, we come through there on our way up to Independence. Missed our boat in Sibley, had to go on upriver to pick up our goods."

The men all gathered around Stagg and squatted or sat on the ground to hear his story.

"Where you headed, Johnny?" Orv asked.

"I—I was going to Bent's Fort."

"Why, that's where we-all's a-goin' ", Early said.

"Yeah, we got some tradin' to do afore we head out for Santa Fe," Lafon said.

"You want to come with us?" Cal asked.

Johnny hesitated. He didn't know these men. They might rob him and kill him. He still had that money the storekeeper in Sibley had paid him. And all of them kept eyeing his papa's rifle.

"I reckon I'll just go on by myself," Stagg said, finally.

"Johnny, you don't want to go anywhere out here by yourself," McTeague said. "Why, you're lucky Old Marsh run up on you."

"Why? Isn't it safe?" Johnny asked.

All the men laughed. Johnny felt embarrassed again.

"Safe?" Cal asked. "Why, it's as safe as sleepwalkin' in a snake den. It's as safe as lightin' up a smoke in a powder factory. Hell, yes, it's safe, what with painted red-skins comin' up on you in the night and cuttin' your throat and takin' your hair home so's the kids can play with it."

"You just as well ride with us, Johnny," Lafon said, some kindness showing in his voice. "As long as you're going that way. There is some safety in numbers. We may not be the best protection in the world, but everyone of us can fight like wildcats when pushed to it."

"I don't know," Johnny said, weighing his choices. He would lose track of Cutter, but that really didn't matter. Cutter was going to Bent's himself. Besides, these men didn't seem all that bad now that he was getting to know them.

"You don't have to make up your mind right away," Orv said. "We're stayin' the night here. You weren't goin' to ride much further today, were you? Light's goin' pretty fast."

Baxter was right. The sun was just touching the horizon. And Johnny had planned to camp by the creek so he didn't run on to Cutter after dark, or have Cutter double back on him with that knife of his.

"I reckon I could stay and ride with you to Bent's," Johnny said.

"Good," Lafon said, slapping his knee. "We get to Bent's, you can get yourself some proper clothes. Injuns there will make you a proper set of buckskins. You got any money?"

Johnny shook his head.

"Well, maybe you can trade one of them pistols for a set of skins."

"Yeah, maybe."

"You can help us get firewood," Cal said. "We eat early and set watches."

"Set watches?" Johnny asked.

"One of us stands guard at night while the others sleep," Early said. "You don't have to take a turn, but you're welcome to."

"I'll take a turn," Johnny said, standing up. Then he turned to Lafon. "Are you going to keep my pistol?"

"Well, for a while, Johnny," Lafon replied. "Until we get to know you a little better. Stagg. That what you said your name was?"

"Yes. John Stagg."

Lafon looked at the other three men, who whispered something to one another, then walked over to Lafon and said something to him that Johnny couldn't hear.

"What is it?" Johnny asked. "What are you whispering about?"

"Oh, nothing," Lafon said. "Only, we heard there was a killing in Sibley the night before we got there. They said a man named Stagg put out the lamp of a man named Maggard. Must have been your pa, huh?"

"My pa was killed by Maggard, sort of."

"What do you mean, 'sort of'?" McTeague asked.

"Nate Maggard was in cahoots with a man they call Cutter. Cutter stabbed my papa in the back."

"We didn't hear all of it, o' course," Lafon said. "But I'd be mighty careful of going back to Sibley."

"Why?"

"Because when we came through, there was talk of getting up a lynching party."

"A lynching party?" Johnny asked. "For who?"

"For someone named Johnny Stagg," McTeague said, looking at Stagg square in the eye.

"Why?" Johnny asked. "I killed Nate in self-defense."

"Well, that's not what they're sayin' in Sibley," Early said. "They said you shot Maggard in the back."

"That's a mighty cowardly thing to do, Johnny," Baxter said. "A backshooter ain't no better'n a damned skunk."

Johnny stood there, looking at the men. He was sure they were going to come at him and kill him right then and there.

13

JOHNNY STARED RIGHT BACK AT THE FOUR MEN.

"I didn't shoot anybody in the back," he said. "Nate was going to shoot me and I shot him. My papa died in my arms right after that."

For a long moment, nobody said a word. The men just glared at Johnny. But he held his ground and didn't avert his eyes nor turn away. He stared right back at them as if daring them to challenge the truth of what he had said.

The men exchanged glances, then shifted their gazes back to Johnny as if trying to make up their minds. Lafon cleared his throat before speaking.

"Out here," Lafon said, "we take a man at his word until he shows us different. There ain't no way to know if you're talkin' with a straight tongue or not, but let me give you a piece of advice, young Johnny."

"I'm listening," Johnny said.

"A man can start fresh out here if he's a mind to, and nobody will think less of him for what he done back in the States. But if he packs his troubles and his bad habits with him, he won't last long. If you're a backshooter, you won't reach Bent's Fort alive. If you're not, you don't have a thing to worry about. Fair enough?"

"Fair enough. And I'm not a backshooter. Nate Maggard was beating my papa to death when Cutter put a knife through his back. If he'd been there, I would have killed him, too, with my bare hands. But he slunk out and I didn't find out until later that he killed my papa."

"That's good enough for me," Lafon said. "What about you boys?"

The three men nodded, but Johnny noticed that their faces were cloudy with doubt. None of them smiled, and it seemed all the friendliness had gone out of them, wiped away by the scowls on their faces.

The men went their ways, and Johnny unsaddled Blue and laid out his bedroll well away from the lean-to. He hobbled his horse and helped gather firewood as the men joked and talked among themselves as if he wasn't even there.

Orville made a fire and Cal filled a pot with water, brought it to the fire ring. Frank and Marsh cut up turnips and potatoes and put some kind of meat into the stew.

"I got buffalo meat, if you need some," Johnny said.

"Cut some up and put it in the pot," Orville said. "That must be what stinks."

Johnny cut up some of the meat packed in his saddle-bags. Lafon watched him and walked over, looked into the open bag.

"What you got in there?" he asked. "What's them papers?"

"It's mostly a book I was reading," Johnny said.

"You can read?"

"Yes, can't you?"

"Why, shore, Johnny. It's just that not many men I know can read or write. What's the book about?"

"It's about a hero named Ulysses and about a bunch of gods."

"Gods?"

"It's a book that was written in Greek and some man turned the words into English."

"I read the Bible once," Lafon said.

"I guess this book was like a Bible to the Greeks. It's full of adventure. Lots of fighting. I think the gods hate Ulysses."

"I knowed a man named Ulysses once't," McTeague said. "He wasn't much of a man. More like a squirrel."

"A squirrel?" Early asked as he put the pot on the fire. The sun had sunk below the horizon and the western sky was filled with painted clouds, all pink and purple and golden.

"He was a shopkeeper back in Virginny, a little weasel of a man who was as jumpy and jittery as a kid with his hand in the cookie jar. He was stealin' his customers blind and I guess he was plumb nervous about it."

Everyone but Johnny laughed.

"Sometimes havin' a big hero's name can make a man mighty small," McTeague said. "I always thought his name should have been Weasel or somethin' like that."

The men all chuckled. Johnny hardly knew what McTeague was talking about.

"The book is called *The Odyssey,*" Johnny said. "And it was written by a poet named Homer."

"Well, now, this here Ulysses, the twitchy little shop-keeper, he should have been named Homer 'stead of Ulysses. Would have suited him more."

"I don't cotton much to either name," Orville said.

"You don't cotton to shopkeepers neither, Orv," Early said.

This time Johnny laughed, too.

The banter continued until supper time, a while after the sun had gone down. Johnny noticed that only three of the men ate together. Early walked around a wide circumference with his pistol and rifle, then came to eat when Baxter had finished and relieved him. They kept the fire low, and none of the men eating looked directly into it.

The stew tasted good, and Johnny ate more than his share. He hadn't realized how starved he was for a complete meal. He had been eating sparse amounts of food while following Cutter, and was always too tired at night to cook much in the way of a meal that would stick to his ribs.

Lafon put out the fire after they had all had coffee, but one man had remained on watch the entire time. Those who were still at the dead campfire pulled out pipes, filled them with tobacco, and smoked them.

"You don't have to stand watch tonight, Johnny," Lafon said.

"Why not?"

"I just think we'd all be more comfortable was you to sleep the whole night."

"You're afraid I might shoot you all in your sleep," Johnny said. It was not a question.

"Now, don't go makin' nothin' out of this what ain't there. It's just that we don't know you well enough yet and we got our own habits."

"Hell, Marsh, you don't even give a man a chance."

"You'll have plenty of chances to prove yourself, Johnny. Out here, all we got is time and you're welcome to your share of it."

Johnny helped clean up the campsite as Early and Lafon tended to the horses and mules. Orville took the first watch. Johnny saw Lafon whisper something to the others just before he went to bed. Johnny was bone-tired and as soon as his eyes closed, he fell asleep. He heard noises during the night, but they were not loud enough to wake him up.

It was still dark when someone shook him awake. He started to say something, but whoever it was put two fingers to his lips, signaling him to be quiet. He shook off sleep and rubbed his eyes. He sat up and felt a hand slide under his arm and lift him to his feet.

It was Lafon. He could barely make out who it was in the darkness. Lafon led him away from the camp before he spoke to him.

"I thought you might want to walk the last watch with me," Lafon said.

"Sure. But you took my rifle and pistol. I won't be much of a guard."

"You won't need them. Come on, let's walk."

He and Lafon walked a wide circle around the perimeter of the camp. Lafon made scarcely any noise, and Johnny tried to walk as softly, but his heavy shoes still crunched on small stones and twigs, much to Johnny's annoyance.

When they were some distance from camp, Lafon stopped and spoke to Johnny in low tones. His voice was so soft, Johnny had to strain to hear.

"Sun'll be up soon," Lafon said. "I been watching you a-sleepin' for quite a spell."

"Why?"

"You can tell a lot by watchin' a man asleep."

"I don't know what," Johnny said.

"Well, for instance, you didn't sleep like no guilty man."

"How does a guilty man sleep?"

"Well, someone your age, if he was troubled, wouldn't sleep very well, I reckon."

"I sleep just fine, Marsh."

"I know. I watched you. Could be those stories about you were all wrong."

"They were."

"Just wanted you to know I'm givin' you the benefit of the doubt."

"Hell, I don't need your damned benefit. I know what happened back in Sibley. I also know there's some awful mean people back there, some boys who don't like me, and maybe some men, too."

"A man can make enemies even if he don't half try," Lafon said.

"I guess that's so."

"Wanted to tell you another thing. Before we go back to camp."

"What's that?"

"Did you notice a couple of horses gone when we left a while ago?"

"I didn't notice."

"Well, it was dark and you wasn't lookin' for anything in particular. But I sent Orv off to check on something for me and my pards, so you won't see him for a while. And Cal is off on another errand."

"Why are you telling me this?" Johnny asked.

"I just didn't want you to be too surprised, that's all."

"I'll bet there's more to it than that."

Lafon chuckled, but said nothing.

"Is that all?" Johnny asked.

"For now. Come on, let's walk another turn and then head back to camp."

Lafon said no more as he and Johnny walked the circle around the camp. They crossed the creek twice and by then, the sky was paling in the east and the stars were fading like the lights of a town going out.

Johnny noticed that two of the horses were gone and there was only one man sleeping, Frank Early. But Frank woke up as soon as he and Lafon approached him.

"Frank," Lafon said.

"Mighty quiet," Early said as he stood up and stretched. "Any sign of them yet?"

"Not yet," Lafon said. "It's too early. Put on some coffee and get out the fry pan. I'll bet Johnny here is hungry."

"Who ain't?" Early said with a grin.

"What did you mean," Johnny asked Lafon, "when you asked if there was any sign of them yet? Were you talking about Cal and Orville?"

"Not exactly," Lafon said. "But we're looking for Orv to ride in any time now."

Johnny noticed that Lafon then looked to the northeast as if expecting Orville to appear on the horizon. He wondered why Lafon had sent Orville off in that direction, if he had. But he knew Lafon was not going to tell him.

Early had the fire going in a few minutes. Johnny gave Blue the last handful of grain he had, and checked his gear. His pistols were still hanging from the saddlehorn. The pistol he had carried was nowhere to be seen, but he figured Lafon had put it under a blanket with his father's rifle. He felt naked without his pistol in its holster, and he wanted to check the powder in all the pans to see if it was still dry. He knew it wasn't. There was dew on the ground from being so close to the creek.

"I'd like to check my pistols and rifles, Marsh," Johnny said when he walked over to the campfire. He could smell the heady aroma of the coffee and his stomach was twisting with hunger.

"Wait'll it gets more light out and Orv gets back. We'll all of us be primin' our smoke poles and pistols."

"Yes, sir," Johnny said, more than a trace of sarcasm in his voice.

Breakfast was not much, but it filled Johnny's belly. Frank fried potatoes and venison left over from the night before, and some dough balls he had thrown in for good measure. These were greasy and so hot they burned Johnny's tongue.

Lafon kept looking off to the northeast the entire time they were eating, and as Johnny was cleaning the fry pan with sand, he heard Frank yell out.

"Here comes Orv," he said. "Over yonder."

Johnny brought the fry pan back and watched as Baxter rode up.

"They'll be here in a half hour," Baxter told Lafon.

"Everybody all right?" Lafon asked.

"They're all fair to middlin'," Lafon said as he swung down out of the saddle.

"Hungry?"

"I ate with them."

"Good. Let's pack it up. We'll leave as soon as they get here."

Johnny started to ask who was coming, but then he saw the wagon train breaking over the horizon. He counted three wagons, some men on horseback.

Lafon turned to Johnny. "Saddle up. We're going to try and make fifteen mile today."

"Who's that?" Johnny asked, pointing.

"Just some missionaries and hunters," Lafon said. "We're leading them to Bent's Fort and then on to Santa Fe."

"How come they don't go with us?"

"Because they got women with them and they have to stop regular. I told them we'd lead them out, but we wouldn't mollycoddle 'em."

One of the riders broke away from the oncoming wagons and rode at a gallop toward their campsite. Something about him looked odd, but it wasn't until the rider rode up that Johnny knew why.

For a long moment, Johnny couldn't believe his eyes. It wasn't a man at all, but a girl, and she had the prettiest face he had ever seen.

"Howdy, Marsh," she said. "Frank."

Then she looked at Johnny with pretty blue eyes that melted something inside him.

"So, you must be Johnny Stagg," she said. "I've got a message for you."

14

JOHNNY ALMOST COULDN'T FIND HIS VOICE. HE POINTED a finger at himself and said, "Me?"

"If you're Johnny Stagg, as Orv said you were, yes," the girl said.

She was wearing a riding dress that was like pants. She didn't ride sidesaddle like most women. And she wore a man's hat and shirt, but now that he could see her close, he saw that the shirt had flowers on it instead of pockets. She was very pretty, about his age, he figured, with long hair in a single braid.

"What's the message?" Johnny asked, still dumbstruck by her.

"Well, I don't want to tell everybody here what it is. You just wait a minute."

She climbed out of the saddle, handed her reins to a grinning Orville, and walked over to Johnny and took him by the arm, led him away from Lafon and Baxter. She was so close, Johnny could smell her perfume. She was tall, but not as tall as he, and she walked fast, with deliberate steps.

When they were out of earshot of the others, she stopped and stood right in front of him, her eyes staring so hard at him he wondered if she was in a temporary trance.

"Do you know a man named Paddy Osteen?" she asked.

Johnny nodded.

"He's my uncle," she said, "and I saw him in Sibley when we passed through. He said that you might be going to Bent's Fort and if I saw you I was to give you a message."

"How would he know I was going to Bent's Fort?"

"He said that after you left, they found some maps among Nate Maggard's things and it appeared he and someone named Cutter planned to go there."

"I reckon Paddy was right."

"He also said that part of the town believed you were a murderer and the other half didn't."

"That sounds about right, too."

"He wanted me to warn you not to come back real soon. He said you might have to wait until the talk died down and cooler heads prevailed."

"That sounds like Paddy. Say, what's your name anyway? I know Paddy had a couple of nieces, one back in Ireland, the other back East somewhere."

"My name's Caitlin O'Brien. My mother is Paddy's sister, and we're from St. Louis. She's with those wagons right back there, along with my father, Seamus. My mother's name is Maureen."

"Why are you going to Bent's Fort?" Johnny asked.

"My father's a trader, and we're actually on our way to Santa Fe. He wants us to live there. He thinks he can make a lot of money buying goods from the Spaniards and shipping them back East and bringing goods from the States to Santa Fe."

"Well, I wish you luck. I don't know anything about Santa Fe."

"Neither do I. My father says that trade will open up

between Mexico and the United States and he wants to make a lot of money."

Johnny wanted to say more, but he heard his name called and just then the wagons were pulling in.

"Time to ride out, Johnny," Lafon called.

"It was nice to meet you, Caitlin," Johnny said.

"Maybe I'll see you at Bent's Fort," she said.

"I—I hope so."

"Be careful. Paddy says a man named Cutter is dangerous and has a friend at Bent's Fort."

"Oh? Did he say who?"

"No. But he said the Maggards know this man, too, and he's very dangerous. So he told me to tell you to watch out for yourself."

"I will," Johnny said.

"I want you to meet my parents, but we probably can't do it now. My father's in a hurry and Mr. Lafon wants to ride ahead. My mother and I are terribly afraid of Indians."

"Well, you be careful, too, Caitlin. I'll be seeing you, I hope."

The people in the wagons lit down, and Johnny tried to see who Caitlin's parents might be, but Lafon surprised him by handing him his rifle and pistol and telling him to "mount up."

"We might see these folks tonight or tomorrow morning, Johnny, so don't go mooning over Caitlin O'Brien."

"I'm not."

"Well, you look like a treeful of owls, boy."

Johnny's face flushed with a rush of blood. He climbed atop Blue and turned to wave good-bye to Caitlin, but she was nowhere to be seen. The next thing he knew, he was following Lafon across the creek, flanked by Baxter and Early, and they were urging him to keep up. He wondered if they were not also guarding him.

Two hours later, McTeague met them on the trail. He

was wearing a wide grin on his face. He waved before they rode up on him.

"What're you grinnin' about?" Lafon asked.

"I was just thinkin' how lucky Johnny is."

"Me, lucky?" Johnny asked.

"Didn't Marsh tell you? I rode over to your tracks and saw who you was a-follerin', that Cutter feller."

"No, he didn't tell me," Johnny said, glaring at Lafon.

"I picked up Cutter's trail and followed him for quite a few miles. Not hard. He's makin' tracks for Bent's Fort, all right."

"Did you see him?" Johnny asked.

McTeague shook his head.

"So?" Lafon asked. "We don't have time to dawdle."

"That Cutter's pretty smart," McTeague said. "If you hadn't run into Marsh here and had follered him, like you was, he'd have probably put your lamp out, Johnny."

"How come?"

"That old boy doubled back and was a-waitin' for you, oh, a good two hours, I figured, from the age of the tracks. He was in a spot where you never would have seen him. And you would have ridden so close to him, you'd have maybe smelled him. But you never would have seen that lead ball a-comin' at you."

Johnny's face drained of color.

"Yep, you can thank Marsh here for savin' your hide. Cutter was gone from his hiding place by the time I come by, but I can tell you I was sweatin' like a horse in the noon sun."

"Well, I guess I owe you and Marsh my thanks," Johnny said.

"You still aim to go after Cutter?" Lafon asked as he kicked his horse in the flanks.

"I won't give up on it," Johnny said.

"It might cost you your life," Lafon said as the others

caught up to him. "A man that sneaky is bound to be hopin' to bushwhack you sooner or later."

"I'll take my chances."

"I'll wager many a man spoke those same words just before takin' his last breath."

Johnny didn't say anything, but he hoped the others couldn't see how badly he was shaking inside. He had no doubt that if he hadn't run into Lafon, he'd be lying dead somewhere and nobody would ever know how he died or where.

15

THEY NO LONGER RODE TOGETHER. AFTER MCTEAGUE'S report of Cutter lying in wait to kill Stagg, Lafon ordered Baxter and Early to act as outriders in case they crossed Cutter's trail. Johnny was grateful and told Lafon so.

"It's not just for your protection," Lafon said. "Cutter just might not be particular who he drops if he sees you with us."

"Just the same, I'm obliged."

"You're turning out to be more trouble than you're worth," Lafon said. "Just keep your eyes peeled and don't ride anywhere near me or the other boys."

"Yes, sir," Johnny said, but there was no sarcasm in his tone. He was just glad he had some company on the journey to Bent's Fort. Even if they didn't like him, it was better than being lonesome or dead.

Johnny watched the sun as they traveled, made notice of the direction they were going. He marveled at all the game they saw; some were animals and birds he had never seen before. They saw small bands of antelope, and flushed prairie chickens and quail. Doves and swifts flew past them, and in the distance, buzzards circled in the sky, small specks that he recognized as those ungainly, ugly birds that fed on carrion. He wondered if the Maggards were still killing buffalo and taking their hides.

When they stopped briefly at noon, Johnny checked the priming on his rifle and pistols. He had noticed that the men he rode with did it on horseback and never missed a step.

"Better throw that meat away you got," Baxter said. "You're attractin' the buzzards."

Johnny looked up and saw a pair of buzzards circling.

"They aren't—"

"Oh, yeah, they are. They're either after that rancid meat you got in your saddlebags or they're speculatin' that you're their next meal."

"That's not funny, Orv," Johnny said.

"No, it ain't. And it warn't meant to be. Them buzzards know who's next to die."

"I don't believe you."

"Ask anybody who's been out on the desert, Johnny."

"Maybe I will."

"Just throw away that meat. Them buzzards are makin' us all nervous."

Johnny threw the buffalo meat away. Orville was right, it was really beginning to get ripe. Even his saddlebags stank of it, and he knew he'd have to do something about them when they stopped that night.

Johnny was hoping they'd rest a while, but Lafon told them to mount up and they were back on the road after stopping for less than fifteen minutes. This time, Lafon and Baxter rode as outriders, while Frank broke trail and McTeague and Stagg rode along together.

"This is a road, isn't it, Cal?" Johnny asked McTeague.

"Yep. Buffler made it, and since then, travelers have used it. See them ruts? Lots of wagons come through here now."

"Are you telling me the buffalo know the way to Bent's Fort?"

"No, but they know the way to water, and rivers is the big highways out here. You follow the buffler and you'll never be far from water. Nor Injuns neither, for that matter."

McTeague thought for a moment. "I would bet hard dollars that Cutter's on his way to Santa Fe like everybody else. He could buy goods cheap there and sell 'em dear in the States."

"No matter where he goes, I'll be right on his tail."

"He must know the country right well. He'll be going slow now, watching out for Injuns."

"That's twice you mentioned Indians. Are we likely to run into them?"

"Likely."

"Friendly ones?"

"Ah, now that's another side of the doubloon, laddie. Some is friendly, and some ain't."

"How can you tell which is which?"

"If their faces are painted and they do a lot of hollerin' and come at you, then likely they're hostile."

"So, if they're not painted, we don't have to worry, right?"

McTeague laughed. "Not always. If we ride across their huntin' grounds and they have a party out after buffler, they're liable to get hostile in a hurry. Injuns don't cotton to ownin' land like we do, but they sure as hell lay out their boundaries when it comes to huntin'. Can't blame 'em really."

"Why not?"

"They been doin' it long enough. Long before the white man come west and started slayin' their game. Seems we kinda cut into their livelihood."

Johnny thought about these things and let his imagination soar as he compared this journey to the one Ulysses made. Ulysses was always running into trouble, and he was far from home, just like Johnny was.

Johnny still had the feeling that he was a prisoner. He couldn't shake it off. He was still trying to figure out Marshal Lafon, who seemed to the be leader, but Lafon was distant, like a man with a lot of secrets.

"You're wonderin' about Lafon?" McTeague said sometime later. The question caught Stagg by surprise.

"How'd you know that?"

"I didn't exactly, but people who first come upon him usually wonder about him after they been around him a while."

"He's your boss, I reckon."

McTeague laughed. "No, we don't have no boss. But he's a wise one, wise to the trail, wise to the ways of Injuns and such."

"You like him."

"I like him some," McTeague admitted. "He kinda grows on you."

"He sure as hell doesn't grow on me."

"I think he's taken a likin' to you, Johnny. Might be he thinks of you as his own son."

"His son?"

"Marsh had a kid, a boy. What are you, eighteen?"

"Nineteen."

"His boy would be about your age now, maybe a couple of years younger."

"What happened to him?"

"Him and his ma, Marsh's wife, was killed by Shawnee back in Ohio a few years back. Some say he never got over it. He's kind of a lone wolf like you."

"My mama died," Johnny said.

"It's different when the ones you dote on are taken from you. Shawnees cut up Marsh's wife and kid pretty bad. Burned him out. The Injuns was drunk and knew he had whiskey. They wanted more and his wife wouldn't give 'em none."

"I feel sorry for him, but that doesn't make me like him."

"Well, like I say, Lafon kinda grows on you. Once you get used to his ways."

"He doesn't grow on me. He isn't anything like my papa. Nobody could replace my papa."

"Kid, that's somethin' you'll likely learn as you grow some more hair."

"What's that?"

"A man's always lookin' for his father, no matter how old he gets. Like they say, it's a wise man who knows his own father."

"That doesn't make sense," Johnny said. "I know who my father is. Was. I don't need to look for another."

"Maybe not. But you'll always be lookin' for the one you lost. Mark my words."

Johnny started to shake his head, but just then, they both saw something far ahead of them.

"What's that?" Johnny asked.

"Looks like Marsh has come up on somethin'. That's him, a-wavin' his bandanna to get our attention."

"Trouble?" Johnny asked.

"Let's go see. Put that blue roan to a gallop."

Before he could react, Johnny saw McTeague kick his horse into a gallop, and by the time he got Blue moving, he was choking on dust.

16

LAFON'S EYES SPARKLED LIKE BLUE FLINTS WHEN JOHNNY
rode up, and his mouth was clenched tight. He was mad
about something.

"What you got?" McTeague asked.

"Follow me," Lafon said, and turned his horse with a
wrench of the reins.

Johnny looked at McTeague, who only shrugged and
put a finger to his lips, signaling not to say anything.

He and McTeague followed Lafon down a little slope
to a small draw where water had washed out some of the
soil. There, in the draw, Baxter lay against the bank, his
eyes closed. To Johnny, he looked dead. As Johnny rode
closer, he saw that Baxter's shirt was soaked with blood
and one arm was tied with a tourniquet made from a bandanna tied tightly and knotted, with a pistol ramrod drawn
through the knot.

"Cal, see what you can do for Orv," Lafon said. "I'm
going to ride up and see if I can spot Frank anywhere.
Johnny, you stay put."

With that, Lafon rode up out of the draw and was gone
before Johnny could get his bearings. McTeague jumped
out of the saddle and knelt down next to Baxter. Johnny

moved Blue closer so he could overhear what the two
might say to each other.

"Orv, is the ball still in you?" McTeague asked. He
leaned over Baxter with his hands poised to peel back
bloody clothing.

"I—I don't know."

"Where are you hit?"

Baxter's face was pale and dripping wet with a sheen
of sweat. His features were contorted in agony. From
where he sat his horse, Johnny thought the ball might have
hit him just below the shoulder, near his heart or in the
left arm. It was hard to tell with all the blood.

"I—my arm hurts like fire, and my chest."

McTeague swore under his breath.

"I'm going to take a look, Orv," he said. "Do you want
a ball to bite on?"

"I already got one," Baxter said. He lifted his head
slightly as if to show McTeague the lead ball in his mouth,
but the effort caused him to grimace in pain.

"Just hold still, Orv. I got to pull back—no, I got to
cut your shirt, maybe the whole sleeve. It's going to hurt
some. Just bite that ball and try not to think of what I'm
doing."

McTeague looked up at Johnny. "I could use some
damned help down here."

"Yes, sir," Johnny said quickly. He slid out of the saddle and let the reins trail. He wasn't worried about Blue
going anywhere. There was plenty of grass in the draw.
He ran over to where McTeague and Baxter were, and
got down on his knees.

"What do you want me to do?" he asked.

"For now, just hold his left hand. Don't squeeze it or
nothin'. Just be ready to grab it and hold it steady in case
I have to go in after that ball. Right now, I'm goin' to
cut that sopping shirt off him."

Johnny watched as McTeague drew his knife. It was a

large one, like the skinners used. Following orders, Johnny gently held Baxter's left hand. The hand was limp. It almost looked as if it was broken, but he knew it wasn't.

McTeague held the bloody shirt with his left hand while he began to cut away the bloodiest part of the shirt that was covering Baxter's chest. The knife was very sharp and the cloth separated easily.

Johnny's stomach knotted up and convulsed when he saw the wound. The bullet hole was plainly visible beneath the sworls of blood on Baxter's chest. It was as black as the bottom of a well and blood was pumping through it with every beat of Baxter's heart.

The hole was in Baxter's chest, not his arm. McTeague turned to Johnny with a look of helplessness on his face. "I'm going to reach around and feel Orv's back," he said. "If there's a hole there, we'll know the lead went straight through."

"If not?" Johnny asked.

"I'll have to probe. It's got to come out, or Orv will die."

Baxter coughed just then and sprayed McTeague's face with pinkish blood and red gouts shot through with white foam. Johnny turned away, but some of the spray struck the side of his face. His stomach roiled with a queasy motion. He had to breathe deeply to keep from getting sick.

"Hold on, Orv," McTeague said. "This is going to hurt some. I've got to move you toward me while I reach around to your back."

"Swallered the ball," Baxter croaked. "When I coughed."

"Well, that won't hurt you. It'll pass."

"Don't make me laugh, Cal."

"Do you want another bullet to bite?"

"Ummm," Baxter said.

McTeague looked at Johnny. "Dig a big-caliber ball out of your pouch and give it to me, Johnny."

Johnny dug in his possibles pouch and felt for the largest ball in there. He brought it up and handed it to McTeague, who rolled it into Baxter's mouth and shoved it up against his teeth.

"Bite down on it, Orv."

Orv wallowed the ball around and got it between his teeth, then bit down on it. His teeth sank into the soft lead. His face twisted in pain and his complexion turned sallow.

McTeague pulled Baxter's upper torso toward him and reached around with his right hand to feel his back. Johnny watched, holding his breath, fearful of what Cal might discover.

"Damn," McTeague said as he gently let Baxter return to his propped-up position against the dirt bank. "The ball didn't come out."

" 'Amn," Baxter said.

"Damn is right," McTeague said. "Johnny, get a fire going real quick. I can handle Orv."

Johnny let out a breath and released Baxter's hand, his mind racing. He looked around for something to burn and saw no wood. His heart sank like a stone dropped in a pool.

"How big a fire do you want?" Johnny asked.

"It don't have to be big, just hot. I'm going to run my knife through it in case I got to cut the ball out of Orv's back."

Johnny looked around and saw some clumps of dried grass. He began jerking these loose from the ground. He made a pile, and then went to his saddlebags and dug into one of them for the loose pages of Homer's *The Odyssey*. He took several of them and began twisting them into tight spirals, which he placed atop the dried grasses as if they were chunks of wood. He had tried to retrieve just those pages he had already read, but there wasn't time to make sure.

He got out his flint and striker from the little tinderbox, and placed these next to the pile of weeds and pages from his book.

"Let me know when you're ready, Cal," Johnny said.

McTeague said nothing, but pushed hard on Baxter's left shoulder to pin him to the bank. Then he pushed his right index finger into the bullet hole in Baxter's chest, very slowly at first. When he had it all the way in, he began to move it. Baxter let out a muffled scream and bit down hard on the lead ball between his teeth.

Then Baxter grunted and slumped over, unconscious.

"Can't find it," McTeague said. He pulled his finger out of the wound and blood gushed out in a flood. McTeague looked at his right arm and saw that it was soaked with blood. And it had not come from the chest wound. Quickly, he cut off Baxter's left sleeve, which was still partially intact, but saturated with fresh blood. "Uh-oh," McTeague said.

"What is it?" Johnny asked.

"Here's another hole, in Orv's arm. He took two bullets. Now, let's hope it went straight through."

Johnny watched as McTeague turned Orv's arm around and bent over to look underneath. He let the arm drop and rocked back on his legs.

"Did it?" Johnny asked.

"Yeah, that one went clean through. But he's lost a lot of blood, and he's losing more by the minute."

"Maybe we ought to pack the wounds and dig out the ball later," Johnny suggested.

"A tourniquet will help stanch the flow of blood from his arm. I'd better get in with the knife and see if I can find the other ball while he's passed out. Get that fire goin', Johnny, and when it's blazin', stick this knife blade in it. I've got to clean this blood off my hands."

Johnny started striking the steel with a chunk of flint, sending sparks into the fine tinder he had nested in the dried grasses. He struck and struck until finally he saw a tiny glow in the shavings. He leaned over and blew gently on the spark until it glowed, pulsing like some miniature orange heart with each breath.

The tinder caught and burst into a small flame. Johnny pushed it deeper into the dried grasses, and then blew on the flames so that they spread. Soon, the grass was alight, and then the twisted pages of the book began to burn slowly. Johnny took off his hat and fanned the flames. He wiped the blade of McTeague's knife on his pants leg, and then thrust the blade into the flames, turning it over and over until the edge started turning blue, then black.

McTeague rubbed his palms and hands on his pants and shirt to dry off the slick blood that covered them.

"It's ready, I think," Johnny said, pulling his hand away from the fire along with the hot knife.

"Help me turn Orv over on his belly," McTeague said. "Then hold him down." He took the knife from Johnny and together, they gently turned Baxter over and laid him out flat facedown.

McTeague straddled Baxter's back and leaned down. He found the entry wound with his left hand and made a mental note of where the ball might have gone. First, he felt Baxter's back, pushing into the flesh with his index finger. The flesh gave, and then he struck a spot where he felt something hard underneath.

"I think I've found where the ball is lodged," McTeague said. "Come over here and hold Orv down in case he wakes up."

Johnny steeled himself and walked over to where Baxter lay with McTeague straddling his back. "Where do you want me to hold him?" he asked.

"Just be ready to push down on his shoulders. Get up there by his head."

Johnny knelt down and sat back on his legs, ready to grab Baxter's shoulders if he tried to get up.

"Here goes." McTeague put his left thumb near the spot where he had felt the hard lump. With his right hand, he put the tip of his knife close to one edge of where he thought the ball was lodged.

Johnny watched as McTeague pushed the knife downward. The tip broke the skin, and blood oozed out. He shoved harder, and the knife parted more flesh. Blood began to gush out more rapidly. McTeague gave one last push, then withdrew the knife blade. He dug inside with his right index finger and curled it around the lead ball. He worked it toward the opening in the skin, digging his finger in even deeper. Finally, when he saw a dark spot, he grasped the lead ball with his thumb and index finger and plucked it out. More blood. Johnny braced himself, but Baxter did not stir.

"There it is," McTeague said, holding up the bloody lead ball. "Slightly flat on one side. Must have hit something either before it went in or after, but I don't think no bones are broke."

"He's bleeding pretty badly," Johnny said.

McTeague grunted and climbed off Baxter's back. He wiped his knife blade on his buckskin trousers and sheathed it. "Get me a canteen," he said. "I'm gong to mix up some dirt and make mud to pack into these holes."

Johnny all too willingly got to his feet and ran over to his horse. He unslung one of his full canteens and brought it back to McTeague, who was digging down under the soil with his knife. He made a concave depression, then took the canteen from Johnny and poured water into the hole. He put both hands in the muck and began to knead the earth and water with his hands.

Johnny watched in utter fascination.

Soon, McTeague scooped up some of the mud with both hands, and carried it to Baxter's back. He pushed mud into the wound he had made, packed it tight, and slapped it solid.

"Now, help me turn him over," McTeague said. "You grab his legs. I'll take the shoulders."

They turned Baxter over and laid him flat on his back.

McTeague crabbed back to the mud hole and scooped up another handful. He was about to fill the entry wound when he paused.

"What's the matter?" Johnny asked.

McTeague said nothing, but leaned over and put his ear to Baxter's mouth. He listened for several seconds.

"Damn, Orv," McTeague said.

"What's the matter?" Johnny asked again.

McTeague looked up at Johnny and shook his head.

"He ain't breathin'," McTeague said.

Johnny felt his legs turn to jelly, and a giddiness assailed him. McTeague and Baxter started to spin around and he lost all sense of direction, just before the world turned black and he felt himself falling.

17

JUST BEFORE HE HIT THE GROUND, JOHNNY GULPED AIR into his lungs. When he hit, he landed on his hands. The fall jarred him back to consciousness, but he felt woozy, light-headed. His hands cushioned the fall, but for a few seconds, he was unable to move.

"What's wrong with Johnny?" Lafon asked as he rode into the draw. "He's not dead, is he?"

"Who?" McTeague asked. "Johnny or Orv?"

"Either damned one," Lafon said, a tone of impatience in his voice.

"I—I'm all right," Johnny gasped. He tried to push himself up, but fell back again on his chest. He rolled over and looked up at Lafon, then at Early, who had ridden up with him. They were both staring down at him with a look that was filled with either pity or disgust.

"Then get up," Lafon said.

Johnny rose to his feet and stood there, teetering on wobbly legs for a minute.

"What about Orv?" Lafon asked.

"I don't think he's breathin'," McTeague said.

He pushed on Baxter's chest as if to make sure, and then started to get up. Before he could make it, Baxter went into a flailing convulsion. His eyes opened wide, and he sat up partly and flailed his arms. He seemed to be trying to suck air into his lungs, but the more he tried to breathe, the more purple his face became.

"He's chokin'," Early exclaimed, as if he was the only one who had his wits about him. "Lord, he's gaggin' on somethin'."

McTeague reached over, grabbed Baxter by the shoulders, and shook him back and forth as if to dislodge whatever it was in his throat.

Johnny raced over and slapped Baxter hard on the back with the flat of his palm, knocking him forward into McTeague. As McTeague tried to push Baxter back away from him, the dying man coughed and spat something up and out of his mouth. Johnny slapped him again, and Baxter gulped in air with a mighty wheeze that filled his lungs.

"He's alive," Early shouted.

"Damned if he ain't," Lafon said.

"But he's bleedin' like a stuck hog, Marsh, looky."

Blood spurted from Baxter's chest and splashed onto McTeague's buckskin shirt. Johnny ran around to the mud, scooped up a handful, slapped it over the hole in Baxter's chest, and pushed him gently down on his back.

"You lie still, Orv," Johnny said as he rubbed the mud into the wound. "Just breathe easy."

McTeague pushed Johnny aside and finished packing the mud into the hole in Baxter's chest. Baxter lay there, his eyes opened wide, breathing like a fish out of water, his chest rising and falling with each breath, his face contorted in agony.

"Well, I'll be damned," Lafon said. "Here I was beginning to think you was a damned jinx, Johnny, and you done saved Orv's life."

Johnny shook his head. He walked over and picked up the object Baxter had spat out of his mouth. He held it up for all to see. "This is a lead ball I put in Orv's mouth so's he could bite down on it when Cal was cutting on him. That's what nigh choked him to death."

Early surprised everyone by swinging his leg over the saddlehorn and jumping down out of the saddle. Then he rushed straight at Johnny, swinging with his right fist. He connected with Johnny's jaw, knocking the younger man down.

"Get up, you sonofabitch," Early said. "I'm going to beat you within an inch of your miserable life."

Early stood there with both fists clenched. Johnny rubbed his jaw, scooted back a foot, and then jumped to his feet. Early cocked another fist, but Johnny waded into him before he could throw a punch and drove a pile-driving right straight into Early's belly, knocking the wind out of him. As Early doubled over, Johnny swung a left hook and smashed Early square in the jaw, knocking his hat off. Early twisted into a half spin from the force of the blow, but recovered quickly.

Before Johnny could get set again, Early barreled toward him, head down. He struck Johnny in the gut and both went down. Johnny wrapped his arms around Early and rolled, trying to get on top of him. But Early kicked out and rolled Johnny back over. Johnny let loose of Early with one arm, and grabbed a handful of Early's hair. He twisted hard, forcing Early's head back. Early knocked Johnny's arm away and tried for a choke hold, but Johnny fended him off with a short uppercut to the chin.

"Frank, stop," McTeague yelled.

"Let 'em be," Lafon said. "Best to let 'em work it out now while the hate's still fresh."

"Johnny don't stand a chance," McTeague said.

"He seems to be holding his own pretty much."

Early tried to bite Johnny's ear, diving for his neck. Johnny moved his head just in time and rammed an elbow into Early's ribs. Early grunted and crabbed sideways to get away from Johnny's grip. Johnny let him go and scrambled the other way, getting to his feet at the same time as Early regained his own footing.

The two men squared off and began circling each other, with Early throwing a fist that Johnny easily sidestepped, or ducked, and Johnny feinting with his left hand, then his right. He watched Early with a focused intensity, searching for any weakness in his attack, for any mistake he might make.

From somewhere deep within him, Johnny summoned a courage he didn't know he had, an instinctive urgency for survival that he had called on before when he faced the town bullies back in Sibley. In fact, as he watched Early, he thought of him as just another one of those boys who had attacked him and torn up his book. He had not come out on top in that battle, but now it was just one on one, and he felt a confidence surge up in him that he had never known before. He didn't hate Early, but he wasn't going to let him grind him into the dirt under his moccasins, and if he was going to go down, he was going to go down swinging—with all his might.

"Come on," Early said. "You little bastard."

"You said the wrong thing that time, Early," Johnny said, and he charged Early with his head up, both arms bent, fists cocked. Early tried to sidestep, and that was his mistake.

Johnny saw the move before Early made it, and met him with both of his feet square on the ground. He loosed a wide swinging right that caught Early in the left ear and rocked him off balance. Early staggered and tried to recover, but Johnny pressed his advantage, stalking in so fast, Early could not defend himself. He tried to lift his arms to ward off the blow he knew would come, but Johnny was too quick and hammered a short hard left to Early's chin, knocking his head back until those watching thought Early's neck would snap.

Then Johnny followed up with another right to the jaw, and a pile-driving left hook that caught Early's head as it was moving from the other blow. The two punches rocked Early, and he dropped his guard as he fought to control rubbery legs and the flashes of lightning in his head.

Johnny pressed his advantage and rammed a straight left fist into Early's midsection, doubling him over and knocking the wind out of him. Johnny then drove a powerful right hand into the left side of Early's face, knocking him down and putting him out cold.

Johnny, panting, stood over his fallen opponent with both fists still doubled up, waiting for Early to show signs of life, or to get back on his feet. But Early did not move.

"That's enough," McTeague said softly. "Early's beaten, Johnny. Pull your horns back in."

"Cal, put out that damned fire," Lafon said as he dismounted. "We'll have every redskin for ten miles comin' to that smoke."

McTeague walked over to the fire and began to kick dirt on top of it. Lafon walked over, leading his horse, to take a look at Baxter. He stood there for a minute or so, then turned to Johnny.

"I don't blame you for this, Stagg," Lafon said. "But by rights, I ought to. Orv's a good man and it looks like he might not make it. But if he does, he sure as hell is going to blame you."

"Why? I didn't shoot him," Johnny said.

"Who did shoot him?" McTeague asked, walking over to stand beside Lafon.

"He didn't tell you?" Lafon asked.

"No."

"He was shot by a man riding a black horse with a blaze face and three or four white stockings."

Johnny's face paled.

Lafon turned his head and looked straight at Johnny.

"You know who shot him, don't you, Stagg?"

"It sounds like Cutter."

"You're damned right. It was Cutter, and if you hadn't been doggin' him all the way out here, this never would have happened."

Johnny balled up his fists again. It wasn't fair, he thought. He was being blamed for what Cutter did to Baxter, but so far, nobody had blamed Cutter for killing his father. The injustice of Lafon's accusation burned at Johnny's sense of fairness like a raging inferno. He wanted to strike out, to hit Lafon the way he had hit Early and make him take back every damned word he had said.

"Sounds to me like you are blaming me for what happened to Baxter," Johnny said.

For a long moment, Lafon said nothing. McTeague shifted the weight on his feet and looked sheepish. Frank Early sat up, holding his head with both hands.

Orville Baxter groaned, opened his glazed eyes, and looked up at the men standing over him. He opened his mouth as if to say something, but no words came out. He blinked his eyes in pain and shuddered deeply as the pain coursed through his body like a river of fire.

"Stagg," Lafon said, "you may not be a jinx, but you're damned sure a cursed man. I said I wasn't blaming you, but maybe I should."

Johnny stood there, the anger in him smoldering like a volcano ready to erupt at any second.

18

Johnny glared at Lafon with a savage intensity. Every muscle in his body quivered with pent-up energy waiting, like a coiled snake, to strike out in self-defense.

"Easy now, Johnny," McTeague said, his voice soft, soothing. "Don't do nothin' you might regret."

"Let him make his move, Cal," Lafon said. "If he means to meet me head-on now, it's better'n waitin' for him to put a bullet in my back."

"I never shot Nate Maggard in the back," Johnny said, seething with anger. "And I wouldn't kill any man over an insult."

"You want to, though, don't you?" Lafon taunted.

"I'll fight you fair, if that's what you want," Johnny said.

"There's been enough fightin'," McTeague said. "Marsh, back off. Johnny, you simmer down yourself. We got a dyin' man here."

Lafon nodded, and a more kindly look crept into his eyes. Johnny unclenched his fists and turned his hands, palms out, to show that they were empty.

"What hit me?" Early said as he struggled to his feet. He wobbled when he tried to take a step. McTeague went over to him and put his arm around his waist to keep him from falling.

"Better take it easy, Frank. You want a swaller of water?"

Early nodded. Lafon let out a breath, then walked over to where Baxter was lying. He knelt down beside him. "Orv, can you hear me?"

"Umm," Baxter moaned.

Lafon turned to McTeague, who was handing Early Johnny's canteen, which he had picked up off the ground. "Can he ride, Cal?"

"I can bandage him up, but it's takin' a chance. He's got four holes in him and the one in his back is pretty bad. He ought to be laid up for a spell."

"Well, bandage him up. I can see he's lost a lot of blood."

"What happened to Cutter?" Johnny asked.

"After he bushwhacked Orv, he lit a shuck," Lafon said. "He's one sneaky bastard. Orv didn't see him until it was too late. There's a creek up ahead and Cutter was waitin' there for you, Stagg." Lafon looked at the wound in Baxter's arm, then at the one in his chest. "I guess he shot Orv in the arm first, and while Orv was tryin' to get his rifle out of its boot, he reloaded and shot him in the chest. Orv said he saw him ride away on that black horse."

"That's him," Johnny said. "I reckon I'll set out after him."

"Your choice," Lafon said.

"I don't think that's too damned sensible," McTeague said.

"Let the bastard go," growled Early. "He's a damned jinx, I told you."

"Frank, just sit down until you get your wits about you," Lafon ordered. "Let's just figger all this out."

"I don't need your permission," Johnny said. "And I'm not wanted here anyway."

Lafon put a hand on Baxter's cheek. It was warm to the touch. Beads of sweat had started to form on Baxter's forehead. Baxter looked up at him and his eyes were cloudy with pain.

Lafon got to his feet as McTeague helped Early sit down against the bank near Baxter. "I'm all right," Early said. "Just a little woozy."

"Then just sit still a while and clear them cobwebs outta your brain," McTeague said.

"The kid knocked me out, didn't he?"

"It was a fair fight, Frank."

"Yeah." He rubbed his jaw and cocked an eye in Johnny's direction. "He's got some bark on him, I reckon."

Lafon and McTeague chuckled.

"Here's the way I see it," Lafon said. "Orv's in a bad way. I don't think he can ride, and we've either got to push on and leave him here for the wagon train to catch up, or all wait for the wagons to come up and see if they can take him under their care."

"He can't ride, that's for sure," McTeague said. "But we'll have to move him out of this draw."

"I agree," Lafon said. "We can carry him to the creek. There's some shade there. So, do we wait for the wagons then? Or one of us stays behind with Orv?"

"I'll stay behind if you want to go on," McTeague said. "Johnny could stay with me if he wants to."

Lafon looked at Johnny.

"I reckon I'll ride on out now," Johnny said. "Go while Cutter's tracks are still fresh."

"Suit yourself," Lafon said.

"I wish you'd stay," McTeague said.

"My mind's made up," Johnny said. "I'll help you move Baxter over to the creek before I go, though."

Lafon started to say something, but bit off the words before they came out. He shrugged and turned his back on Johnny. McTeague jumped into the breach. "We could use your help, Johnny."

Lafon turned to Early. "Have you got back your senses yet, Frank?"

"I can ride," Early said.

"Take the horses out of the draw and walk 'em to the creek over by those cottonwoods. I'll help Cal and Johnny carry Orv up there."

Early rose to his feet. He was more steady this time, but he staggered a little as he started to grab up the horses one by one.

"Orv here was just a kid," McTeague said to Johnny, "when he fought with Andy Jackson down in New Orleans. He never got a scratch, but he was right in the thick of it. Came down from Kentucky with Andy's boys."

"I'm sorry he got shot," Johnny said.

"Can you take his legs?" McTeague asked. "I'll take his shoulders and, Marsh, you can kind of guide us out of here, maybe hold up the middle."

Lafon and Johnny took their positions after McTeague stood next to Baxter's head. "Ready?" McTeague said. "Let's do 'er."

The three men bent over and grabbed Baxter, lifted him from the ground. He opened his eyes and groaned. Early walked away, leading the horses out of the draw as the three men began carrying Baxter out.

Ten minutes later, they laid Baxter by the creek, in the shade of two cottonwoods. He had passed out again, but the mud had stopped the bleeding. Only a few drops leaked out of his wounds.

"I'll get some creek mud," McTeague said. "It'll work better. And I'll bind him up. Frank, Marsh, give me your bandannas."

Johnny stood there awkwardly, watching as Lafon and Early untied their bandannas and handed them to Mc-Teague. Then he went to his horse.

"I'm going back to the draw for my canteen," he said. "I'll fill it here and then be on my way. I'll say good-bye when I'm ready to leave."

"You don't need to say good-bye," Early said. "Good riddance, I say."

"Well, then, I won't say good-bye. Maybe I'll see you all at Bent's Fort."

"If you make it that far," Early said.

"I'll make it."

"Not if Cutter cuts you down, you won't."

"That's enough, Frank," McTeague said. "Johnny, I hope we run into you again. Do you even know the way to Bent's Fort?"

"No, but Cutter does. I'll find it."

"Just head southwest until you hit the Arkansas River, then follow it on a northwest heading. It'll be the first big river you see."

"Thanks, Cal," Johnny said.

Lafon stepped forward. He held out his hand. "No hard feelin's?"

"Nope," Johnny said. "I thank you for letting me ride with you. I won't forget you."

He was starting to choke up, but he shook Lafon's hand. Then he mounted his horse and gave a wave as he rode off.

"I hope Orv gets better," he said.

"You'll find Cutter's tracks off yonder," Lafon said, pointing to a place beyond the creek. "I hope you get him before he gets you."

Johnny said nothing. He rode back to the draw and found his canteen. It was almost empty. But he rode to the creek a different way, so that he would not have to see Early again and perhaps get into an argument.

It was late in the day when Johnny filled his canteen, and he knew he'd have to hurry if he was going to pick up Cutter's trail before sunset. He knew he was taking a chance going after him alone. Cutter was far more dangerous than he had realized, and he knew he'd have to be careful. He thought of Orville Baxter, a seasoned fighter evidently, and how Cutter had shot him from ambush. The same thing could happen to me, he thought.

Maybe Cutter was waiting somewhere at that very moment, waiting to shoot anyone out of the saddle who might be following him.

When he found Cutter's tracks a half hour later, he saw how fresh they were. Less than three hours old. Johnny's heart pounded at the thought that Cutter was not far ahead of him. He stopped for a moment and looked back toward the creek he had left not long before.

Perhaps, he thought, he should have stayed with Lafon and the others. It would have been safer. But he no longer felt welcome in their company. A man had to move on, follow his own path, he knew. He had been distracted by running into Lafon and the others, and it might have cost the life of Baxter. He would not make that mistake again.

Still, he would have liked to have been at the creek when the wagon train pulled up. Then he could have seen Caitlin O'Brien again and they could have talked about her uncle, Paddy Osteen, a man he missed very much at that moment. He tried to picture Paddy taking care of his father's blacksmith shop, but even as he turned his horse to go on, the memory of Paddy's puckish Irish face was beginning to fade from memory.

But he remembered Caitlin's face, how pretty she was. Would he ever see her again? Would he ever see Paddy again? Or Phill Hardesty, or Mrs. Coombs?

He rode on, into the sunset, following the trail of the man who had murdered his father, and he had no answers. Only questions.

Only questions, and a deep fear of what lay ahead.

19

Sometime during the night, Johnny awakened to the sound of distant thunder. When he opened his eyes and looked up at the sky, the stars were still out and he felt relieved. Then a moment later, he saw lightning to the west, jagged streaks of quicksilver illuminating massive black clouds. And then the wind struck his face, brisk and chill, and he knew the storm was blowing his way.

He had followed Cutter's tracks until it got too dark to see, and had then ridden off the trail to a protected place, covering his tracks. He had laid out his bedroll and gone to sleep without eating anything. Now he was hungry and dismayed that it was still dark. He knew he had gained some on Cutter, but not enough.

Now, if it rained, Cutter's tracks would be washed away. He might still pick up the trail if he looked hard enough, but it would be a slow and painstaking task. It was still too dark to even think of picking up the trail again, and from the looks of the clouds and the lightning, before long he'd be wet and miserable. He mentally cursed the fact that he had no slicker.

The first thing he thought of as the thunderclaps grew louder was to take care of his pistols and his father's Lancaster rifle. He got up and walked over to where he had laid out his saddlebags. His father's pistol was inside, and Nate's, but his own was still in its holster, underneath his bedroll. He put the holster in the saddlebags, wrapped both pistols in cloth. He stuck his own pistol inside his belt and put his shirt over it. It would get wet, like his rifle, but when the rain passed, he would oil the locks and recharge the pans when they were dried.

He dug out some jerky he still had left and a moldy piece of bannock. He chewed on those and watched the storm head his way. The lightning exposed the bulging black clouds, laced them with quicksilver. And now he could smell rain, could taste the faint moisture in the air. Soon, he knew, he and Blue would be drenched. The horse was already nervous and fidgety, pawing the ground as if to loosen his hobbles, and his hide quivered with every clap of thunder.

Johnny walked over and patted Blue on his withers to calm him down. Then he saddled the horse quickly. He did not want to be on the ground when the rains came, and he wanted to take his bearings before all of the stars disappeared.

Johnny rolled up his bedroll last and secured it behind the cantle. He set a course to the southwest, guided by the stars still overhead, mainly Polaris, which still shone bright in Ursa Minor. He gave no thought to finding Cutter's tracks in the dark, but he hoped he didn't stumble over the man by accident.

Johnny mounted up and continued to pat Blue to give him reassurance as the loud thunder increased and the lightning danced closer. The storm was blowing down on him from the northwest, and he knew there was no way to escape it. The wind blowing against his face told him that much, and now the air was thick with moisture, almost like a heavy dew. He felt the wetness on his face and hands, and Blue's hide was getting slick where it was exposed.

The wind struck before the rain began, slamming into Johnny and his horse with a fury that whipped his clothes and tossed Blue's mane and tail with violent gusts. Johnny bent over and held onto the saddlehorn, turned his head to try to shield his right cheek from the stinging spray of grit and sand. By then, the sky was full dark and the stars had disappeared under a layer of bulging, elephantine clouds that made the dark of the night even darker.

The wind increased in intensity, and Blue staggered under the brunt of its violent assault. The horse kept wanting to turn its rump to the wind, and Johnny knew that would have been the sensible thing to do, but to allow Blue to do that would push them both way off their heading for Bent's Fort.

So Johnny bent his horse and himself into a quartering path against the slash and whip of the wind as lightning flared in the sky to the north and spread to the south, as if to block his way. And the thunder cracked like a thousand cannon all firing at once, or like a phalanx of rifles all triggered at the same time as if some general stood on a hidden hill ordering an attack on the valley below.

When the rains came, they came in a blistering torrent and shrank the land to nothingness, so that he could not see beyond the back of Blue's head, and the rain needled him more fiercely than the sand had stung him, tore at his eyes until he was even more blinded and could see nothing, unless he wished to go blind from the pelt of water against the naked orbs in their red-rimmed sockets. Indeed, those first lances of hard rain rawhided his eyes until he thought they must be bleeding down his wind-wounded cheeks.

Johnny pulled his hat down tight and prayed for a shelter that he knew was not there. There was water everywhere and in everything and Blue was at a walk, struggling against the brutal wind, tossing his head as if to shake off the raindrops, and probably blinded, too, as if his eyes had been stung by a thousand bees.

So horse and man wandered aimlessly along some unknown course through blistering sheets of rain, their forms lit by splashes of ragged lightning that laddered crazily down from the sky, the thundering so close it deafened them before it pealed across the sky in a rumbling that sounded like huge temple pillars crashing down from Samson's great strength and anger, and there was no respite, no ceasing of the rain and the wind, and horse and man were lost in a raging sea that sent giant combers crashing against their frail bodies, so twisted and angled out of logical proportions by the sizzling light that illuminated only more darkness and more rain, as the wind snatched their breaths away and filled their mouths and nostrils with drowning gobbets of water.

And still Johnny rode on, Blue barely moving forward against the wind and the lancing rain, lost in some tunnel of rage, deep in a cave of storms that grew darker, even with the fractured spears of lightning that struck land and rock with bolts of electricity that fried the air and left the taste of pennies in his mouth and his skin tingling underneath, as if it had taken on a charge from the magnetized air.

Johnny lost all track of time during that first onslaught of the storm. He did not know if it was night or day, and he didn't much care. He was cold and wet and lost, and the world he had known was no longer friendly. He gasped for breath and spoke to his horse, but even he could not hear his words in the howl of the wind and the rattle of rain. He thought of dismounting and squatting underneath Blue for shelter, but he had not the strength to dismount, and might never find a way to climb back into the saddle. Every muscle and bone in his body shrieked with pain, as if he had been hammered by a multitude of faceless demons borne out of the night by some invisible force.

It seemed like hours had passed when Johnny first noticed that the sky was no longer so dark nor the wind so strong. The rain still came down in drenching torrents, but the wind had slackened enough so that he could open his eyes and see the graying sky in the east.

Gradually, the light spread to the rest of the sky, a pale, ghostly, gray light that was eerie as it painted the land a somber hue. Now he could see the raindrops strike the ground, which was covered with a thin lake of water, so that each drop made a splash and the water rippled until it was like that in a boiling kettle. *Spank, spank, spank.* The raindrops made their own tattoo, plinking and plunking a kind of strange music like none he had ever heard before.

Small rivers ran everywhere and there was no trail, just flattened grasses and miniature torrents snaking through the clumps, and where Blue walked, he left mud in his wake, and Johnny could tell by the way the horse walked that he was tired, so weary he could barely make headway.

And the sky was so bleak, Johnny could get no bearings. There were no landmarks that he knew or could fathom, and he hoped he was still heading to the southwest. At least he had the eastern sky for a time to give him that mooring to reality, but after a time, there were only gray clouds from horizon to horizon, and no markers of where he had been nor where he was going.

On, ever on he rode, across the trackless waste, as the skies sobbed and bled their tears on him with an incessant tattering of sound on his hat and saddle, and he silently pleaded for relief from the relentless downpour. He shivered even though he was warmer now than he had been during the night. His toes were numb, without feeling, and his fingers were useless appendages, the skin all wrinkled like colorless prunes.

His clothes were plastered to him like a second skin, and there was not a dry spot on his body. He felt miserable. Hunger gnawed at him like some beast deep inside his stomach, and his eyes were raw from trying to see in the dark and from the nettles the rain had flowered on his lids and even inside his sockets.

By late afternoon, the rain had almost stopped, but the land was soggy and there were great swatches where sudden floods had washed away the soil and all its battered vegetation.

He rode on into the evening, and there was no sunset to be seen beyond the thick gray ceiling of clouds that hid the heavens and turned the harsh land bleak and bereft of all life, all reason for living.

20

THEN CAME THE LONG DAYS OF WANDERING LOST, THE nights of cold that seeped into the bones, and the land broken and ditched and rumpled, with small mesas and plateaus and rocks that towered like ancient statues turned to rust with the red of iron in them the color of dried blood.

The rain had washed the land of those who had made tracks upon it, and left swirls of mud and sworls of sand like puzzling scrawls made by some giant footless beast that slithered in corkscrew undulations as if it were serpentine and eyeless, as aimless as Johnny and his disconsolate blue horse.

But he was wending his way to the south and west, and something inside him drove him to go on and find his way in an alien world where things grew that he had never seen before, and when he did, one day, find tracks, find signs of human beings, a fear came into him that made him check his powder and reseat the ball in his pistol and the one in his rifle. For these were pony tracks and they were made by unshod stock, deep enough to tell him that they were ridden by men with copper skins, not just stray horses gone wild.

But Johnny saw no man, white or red as the iron in the earth, and his canteens drained day by day and drop by drop, and Blue foraged on tough grasses that were already bleached by a relentless sun burning in its summer cauldron down a cloudless blue sky scrubbed clean of clouds by the caustic wind that blew across the plain, carrying grit and sand in its teeth.

He ate jackrabbits and shot an antelope one day, the meat so tough he could barely chew it, and yet it sustained him for more days until it turned rancid in his saddlebags and on the horse's rump, until he had to throw what was left of the carcass away to feed the buzzards that were now following him as if he was leading them through these desolate places.

Came the day then when Johnny, his last canteen nearly empty, his rib bones showing beneath parched skin, with Blue gaunt and lean as a whippet, rode up on a river so wide it must be the Arkansas. The river, too, was the color of the land, a muddy rusted hue like the iron-laden buttes and spires that jutted up as if remnants of some prehistoric civilization gone extinct millions of years before, wiped out by plague or catastrophe, or a flood of awesome proportions.

Johnny and Blue drank from the river and drew some vitality from its warm waters, which were yet cooler than the air and the rising heat from the ground. Johnny filled his canteens and wondered if now he might follow the river westward and find Bent's Fort, find Cutter and draw from him blood in payment for the murder of his father.

He followed the river then, taking game from its banks in the mornings and evenings, letting Blue graze on the lush grasses that grew along its wending course, finding shade in the cottonwoods when the sun became too hot to bear. He loved the river so much he almost forgot his reason for being there, almost forgot where he hoped it would lead him. After the trek across the merciless plains,

the river was like an Eden to him, a paradise where he
wanted not, needed not, and he would have been content
to stay there until winter. He waded it, swam it, rode Blue
through it, romped on its sandbars, dove wide-eyed
through its depths, bathed in it, baptized himself in it until
he felt whole again, nourished by some mysterious substance in its depths, something that fed his soul and healed
his tormented body with an invisible, soothing balm. The
river was his savior, his eternal salvation, and he emerged
from it a changed man, much grown, much alive in a way
that he had never been before.

But one day, not long after he found the river, he
rounded a bend and saw, through the trees, teepees and
white men's tents nestled in a shady grove, and he thought
his heart had stopped, so great was his joy and surprise
at seeing signs of habitation.

As he rode closer to the encampment, he saw an even
more marvelous sight off to the right, on the plain, a huge
structure that appeared to have been made out of mud.
But he knew it was a fort because of its parapets and high
walls and a lookout tower. There was an American flag
high atop a pole next to the lookout keep, flapping in the
breeze as if a sign of welcome to those who came from
a foreign land.

Johnny's heartbeat quickened as he rode toward the encampment, where now he saw wagons and dogs and chil-
dren playing, smoke rising from cookfires, racks filled
with strips of meat and sides of fish, hides stretched on
willow withes, and Indians wearing feathers and beads
and buckskins.

Johnny rode into the encampment, which stretched
along a wide bend of the river. No one challenged him,
and it made his heart swell as if he was a part of all this,
as if somehow those who looked at him saw who he was
and accepted him without question.

He was going to turn toward the fort when he saw the

wagons lined up between the fort and a small camp somewhat separated from the rest of the people. He passed two men chiseling out a cottonwood to make a dugout canoe, and they waved to him. He smelled the meat on the drying racks and saw buffalo hides staked out, drying in the sun. At the little camp where the wagons were, he saw Caitlin O'Brien and he waved to her. He was not surprised when she smiled at him and waved back.

"We wondered what had happened to you," she said when Johnny rode up. "My father said that you were surely dead. But Marsh said you'd be hard to kill."

"Lafon said that?"

"And Cal McTeague, too. Are you just going to sit on your horse all day, Johnny? I offer you the hospitality of our camp."

Johnny managed a sheepish grin and climbed down from his horse. Blue whickered when Caitlin walked up. She rubbed Blue's nose. The horse whinnied.

"He likes you," Johnny said.

"You look like a beggar man," she said. "Whatever happened to you?"

"I got lost," he said. He looked around, but saw no one he knew.

"Where is everyone?" he asked.

"Oh, were you expecting a welcoming committee? I thought you were coming up to see me."

Johnny could not keep from blushing. "I—I just wondered if, well, where everybody was."

"I wished you had stayed with Marsh and the others. I was disappointed when we came to that creek and found out you were gone. That wasn't very nice of you."

"I had to leave, Miss O'Brien."

"Please, call me by my name, Caitlin. I was hoping to see you again, and when Cal told me you had ridden off, well, I was just brokenhearted."

"You were?"

"Yes. My uncle Paddy told me I'd like you when I met you, and he was right."

"You're embarrassing me, Miss . . . ah, Caitlin."

"Good, I like that in a man. Are you hungry?"

"Some, but I . . ."

"If you're looking for that Cutter fellow, he's gone."

"You saw him? Here?"

"No, but I heard Marsh talking to Orv about him."

"Orv? He's still alive?"

"He says you saved his life. He wants to thank you."

"I almost killed him, you mean. He nearly choked to death on a rifle ball I gave him."

"Look, Johnny, you should go over to the fort. That's where Marshal and the others are right now. But first, why don't you unsaddle your horse and put him in that rope corral yonder and I'll give him some grain. Both of you look half-starved."

Johnny laughed as he looked at where Caitlin was pointing. There were horses and mules and two hollowed-out sections of cottonwood that looked like feed and water bins.

"All right," he said, "I'll do that. By the way, did you see some men bring in those buffalo hides that are drying out there?"

"Johnny, you're full of questions that I can't answer. I've been busy. We're going to leave for Santa Fe in two or three days and I've got a lot to do. I hope you'll have supper with us tonight."

"I will if I'm welcome," he said.

Caitlin smiled, then stepped forward and wrapped her arms around Johnny, squeezed him tightly. Then she pecked him on the cheek, making it turn rosy once again.

"Does that answer your question?" she said.

"Yes'm. I mean, uh, yes, I'd be pleased to take supper with you. I just didn't know if Marsh . . ."

"Oh, go on, will you? I'll unsaddle your horse and put him up. You're as fidgety as a long-tailed cat in a room full of rocking chairs."

They both laughed.

"I guess I don't need to take my rifle to the fort," he said.

"No," she said. "Not unless you plan to shoot someone. Do you?"

"I reckon not."

"I'll take care of everything," she said. "I've learned a lot on this trip. That horse won't bite, will he?"

"No'm, I mean, no, he's never bitten anyone. And he likes you."

"What's his name?"

"I call him Blue."

"That's a suitable name," she said. "Now, you go on. And take a bath while you're in Bent's, unless you'd rather soap up in the river just wearing your birthday suit."

"I reckon I can take a bath in the fort."

"And shave that beard off," she added. "Your whiskers scratched my face when I kissed you."

Embarrassed, Johnny stared down at his feet for a moment, then smiled. "I'll scrape my face."

"Don't drink too much with those rough men," she said as Johnny started walking toward the fort. "I want you to taste my cooking."

"I won't," he said. She waved at him and he waved back.

He hoped she hadn't heard his heart pounding. When she kissed him on the cheek, he'd thought the damned thing was going to burst out of his chest.

Caitlin O'Brien, he thought, was the most beautiful woman in the world. And, he was sure, she liked him.

He knew that he liked her.

"Paddy, you were right," he said to himself aloud. "Your niece is a beauty."

He almost danced the rest of the way to the fort. He felt so light, he wondered if he had any weight to him at all.

21

JOHNNY PASSED MEN COMING AND GOING FROM THE fort as he walked to the entrance. His eyes widened when he saw Indians of various tribes, bearded men speaking French or Spanish. As he walked through the entrance beneath the bell tower, a host of aromas assailed his nostrils, and he overheard conversations in several languages. Men came and went from small rooms, and the hubbub inside attested to the busyness of the fort. He smelled hay and cooking meat, the scents of livestock and pipe smoke.

Bewildered, Johnny stood there for a long time just marveling at the polyglot of conversations and the variety of men inside, all of whom ignored him as they spoke, gestured, and smoked. He thought he could smell the aroma of rum coming from somewhere, and there were noises coming from the second floor, the clink of pewter tankards and the roar of laughter. He didn't see a familiar face anywhere.

He walked along the row of rooms and looked in, but saw no one he knew. The strongest smells of animals came from the back, and when he went there, he saw cattle and sheep feeding on the hay of cut grasses.

He walked back into the main room on the first floor,

conscious now of his own tattered clothing, his worn-out
boots, eaten away from inside by his sweat and from the
outside by wind and rain and grit. Here, inside, were men
in buckskin finery, with beaver hats and clay pipes and
elegant beaded possibles pouches and powder horns with
scrimshaw drawings, boot moccasins with thick soles and
heavy laces.

When he had ridden through the camps along the river,
he had looked for Cutter's black horse and the horses he
had seen the Maggards riding, but had not seen them, nor
any animal that looked familiar. Now he found himself
studying the faces of trappers and Indians, knowing that
it was very unlikely that he'd see anyone he knew, unless
it be the men who had befriended him weeks before. Caitlin had said that Marshal and the others were inside the
fort, but it was a huge edifice and they could be anywhere.
He entered a room where some trappers were sitting
around, smoking their pipes. One or two were conversing
with Indians in sign language.

"I'm looking for Marshall Lafon," Johnny said.

One of the men stopped talking and looked at Johnny
with a facial expression that obviously reflected his irritation. He poked up his thumb and lifted it in a sign that
meant "upstairs."

"Thank you kindly," Johnny said.

There was a wooden and adobe staircase at the end of
the large room and men were going up and down it.
Johnny ascended to the upper level and saw more rooms
without doors. He heard conversation and noises from one
of them and headed there. He smelled tobacco smoke and
rum and heard the *snick, snick* of cards being dealt and
the clack of coins.

He entered the room, feeling like an intruder, but also
oddly at home. It wasn't like the tavern in Sibley, but
men were smoking, drinking, talking, and laughing. A pall
of blue-gray smoke hung in the air like a thin shawl. It

was darker than outside, and it took him a moment to adjust his eyes to the light.

"Well, well, well, looky who's here," Lafon said in a loud voice.

Johnny saw him then, standing over a table, watching a game of four-card monte. The men were choosing from a deck of Spanish playing cards. Lafon beckoned for Johnny to come over. Against the wall, Johnny saw Frank Early, frowning as he smoked his pipe. He didn't see McTeague or Baxter just then, but the room was crowded.

"Thought you was wolf meat by now, Johnny," Lafon said.

"I'm here."

"And so you are. Were your ears burning?"

"What do you mean?"

"We've been talking about you ever since you left us at the creek."

"I've got some questions to ask you, Marsh, if you're not too busy."

"Sure, but first you've got to see Orv. He wants to tell you something."

"Where is he?"

"Over yonder, with Cal."

"I saw Early. He looks like he's still mad at me."

Lafon laughed. "I don't know. He don't talk about you much. Follow me."

Baxter and McTeague were in a corner talking to another man. When Johnny and Lafon walked up, Baxter's eyes widened. His left arm was in a sling and there was a bandage on his chest that showed under his buckskin shirt.

"Well, piss my britches," Baxter said, "if you ain't a sight for sore eyes."

"Hello, Orv. I'm glad to see you looking fit," Johnny said.

The man standing with Baxter and McTeague turned

around and looked at Johnny. Their eyes met, but Johnny did not recognize him. He wore no hat and his hair was cut short, and it was carrot-colored. Unlike the others in the room, he was not clad in buckskins, but wore dark trousers and a chambray shirt, shiny military boots, a wide belt with a large square buckle. He held a pewter tankard in his hand and was leaning against the wall.

McTeague grinned and stuck out his free hand. He, too, had a stein in his fist.

"Johnny, as I live and breathe," he said.

"No," Baxter said, "as *I* live and breathe." Then he turned to the man next to him and said, "Seamus, this is the lad I told you about, the one who saved my life."

"You must be Johnny Stagg. I'm Seamus O'Brien. Caitlin's father. I must say, I've heard a lot about you, from my brother-in-law, Paddy, from Cal, Marsh, Orv, Frank, and my daughter, Caitlin."

"Yes, sir," Johnny said, shaking O'Brien's hand. "I'm pleased to meet you."

"You seem to be a man full of contradictions," O'Brien said, looking at Johnny straight in the eye.

"I don't know what you mean, sir."

"According to some accounts, you're a strange man. Some say you're a backshooter, a drifter, a man born for the rope or the bullet. Paddy says you've got high morals. Others think you're bad luck, a killer with a notorious past and no future. Caitlin thinks you're nice. I don't know what to think, looking at you."

"Think what you want, Mr. O'Brien. My father was murdered by two men. I killed one of them when he tried to kill me. I'm after the other man, who stole my father's money and stabbed him in the back."

"That's something the law should take care of."

"What law is that, Mr. O'Brien?"

"Civilized law, young man. The law that keeps us all from being savages."

"And where was that law when Cutter shoved a knife in my father's back and stole my papa's savings?"

"I'm sure there's law in Sibley."

"Cutter's not in Sibley," Johnny said. "And I don't see any law out here on the frontier."

"It will come. You must be patient. You shouldn't take the law into your own hands. A man who lives by the gun will die by the gun."

"I thought it was a sword."

"So, you can read, can you?"

"And write, too," Johnny said.

"Then you should take up a profession. Make something of yourself."

"That's what I aim to do, sir. But Cutter has to pay for what he did, and he will."

"I'm going to give you some advice, Stagg. Stay away from my daughter. You seem to have a knack for getting into trouble. I won't have her life ruined by someone so bent on vengeance, he leaves his home and takes up the gun. I think you're going to wind up being an outlaw."

"Seamus," McTeague said, interrupting, "Johnny's just doing what any man would do who has been wronged."

"He's taking the law into his own hands, Cal. Vengeance is mine, saith the Lord."

"Mr. O'Brien," Johnny said. "A man named Nate Maggard pistol-whipped my papa near to death. Cutter finished it when he put a knife in my papa's back. I didn't see the Lord there when my papa died."

"He'll be there when Cutter dies," O'Brien said.

"I hope so, sir. Because Cutter's surely going to die for what he did."

Lafon stepped in then, coming between Johnny and O'Brien. "Let's all cool down," he said. "We can continue this argument some other time. Johnny, have a drink."

"I don't want one, Marsh. I want to know if you've seen Cutter or the Maggard brothers."

"They were here," Baxter said before Lafon could answer. "Left two days ago. The Maggards sold their buffalo hides and bought goods to sell in Taos and Santa Fe."

"I'll be leaving then," Johnny said, "as soon as I buy some clothes and supplies."

"There's something you ought to know, Johnny," Lafon said. "Before you go off half-cocked."

"What's that?" Johnny asked.

Before Lafon answered, he looked at Baxter and McTeague. Both men nodded.

"Cutter got here to Fort William first. He met a man named Mike Purdy. Purdy's someone we know. He's bad medicine."

"I never heard of him," Johnny said.

"He's a big man," McTeague said. "Big and mean. We ran across him in Taos last year when we come down from the mountains. He killed two men in Taos and another in Santa Fe."

"For no good reason," Baxter said. "Johnny, you won't stand a chance against Cutter now that he's hooked up with Mike Purdy."

"Orv's right," Lafon said. "So, I've got an offer for you."

"Better listen to him, Johnny," O'Brien said. "Marsh knows men. He's agreed to work for me when we settle in Santa Fe. All of these men will be rich very shortly. You could do yourself some good if you work as hard as they do and keep your nose to the grindstone."

"Johnny," Lafon said. "There's a fortune to be made in fur trapping and trading. O'Brien here has the contacts in St. Louis and back East."

"I know there's money to be made in furs," Johnny said. "But—"

"Johnny," Lafon interrupted, "you are, by God, green as a gosling and soft as a boilt turnip, but I'll make a beaver trapper of you if you come with us to the Shining

Mountains. Forget about Cutter and the Maggard brothers. Make your mark on life. Come with us. Men like Cutter and Purdy aren't worth getting killed over. Someone will kill them one day, you can bet on it."

Johnny drew in a deep breath, held it. He looked at the men standing around him. He looked at McTeague and then at Baxter; then lastly he looked at O'Brien. He let his breath out before he turned back to Lafon.

"My papa told me, more than once, that there was a right time for everything a man might want to do. He said, 'To all things there is a season.' I put a lot of stock in things my papa told me. I think there's a reason for everything and a learning in everything a man does, good or bad. I came out here with a purpose and a reason. I aim to follow through on what I mean to do. After that, there'll be another season and another time. Something's pulling at me to get justice for my father. He meant a lot to me. He means a lot to me now. I owe him for his teachings and what he gave me."

"You mean the money that was stolen," O'Brien said.

"No, I mean the things he gave me to learn for myself. And one of those was how to make my way in the world, on my own. One thing none of you knows is that if I let this go, if I don't go out and meet my troubles head-on, they'll surely be my troubles for the rest of my life. Nate Maggard had three brothers. I think they mean to kill me because I killed Nate in self-defense."

"You don't know that for certain," Lafon said.

Johnny shook his head. "No, I do know it for certain. If I don't do this, I'll always be looking over my shoulder. I'll always be watching for one, or all, of those men to come after me because of what I did and for what Cutter and Nate did."

"You're just looking for trouble," O'Brien said. "And you're sure as hell going to find it."

"I already have, Mr. O'Brien."

"Sleep on it, Johnny," Lafon said. "I think you'd make a hell of a mountain man, a hell of a trapper."

"Maybe," Johnny said, "but I'll come to that in good time, if that's my destiny. And I thank you for asking."

"Johnny," McTeague said, "you were chasing one man. Now there are five of them, with Purdy and the Maggards. Those are not good odds. Five to one."

"No, I suppose not. But it's something I have to do."

"Are you bound to go after them then?" Baxter asked. "Right now?"

Johnny looked at O'Brien. "Mr. O'Brien, I saw Caitlin. She invited me to supper tonight."

"She's just a child who doesn't know her own mind. I won't have a man like you sitting at my table, Stagg."

"I'll tell her that when I go to fetch my horse, Mr. O'Brien. I think I'd choke on my food if I had to eat with a man like you."

With that, Johnny turned on his heel and walked across the room. He stopped in front of Frank Early and smiled.

"Well, are you going to throw in with us, Stagg?" asked Early. "Did Marsh make you an offer?"

"He did, and I turned him down."

"I knew you was no good, Stagg."

"I guess I wouldn't need any enemies if I had you as a friend, Frank, would I?"

Before Early could answer, Johnny was gone. He went downstairs and stopped the first man he saw.

"Where can I buy some buckskins and moccasins and get a bath and a shave?" Johnny asked.

The man, a burly bearded man in buckskins, pointed to a room near the door.

"That's the trading room, sonny," he said. "You can buy most anything you need in there."

"Thanks," Johnny said. "I'm much obliged."

"Don't pay the first price you hear from the traders. They'll know you're a greenhorn and try to make you pay dear. They'll respect you if you don't bite at the first hook they drop into the water."

By the time Johnny left the fort, he was wearing buckskins and moccasins, and had a spare set of each. He had a razor and soap, and headed for the river, well downstream from the camps. He had traded his old clothes and worn-out boots to a Southern Cheyenne with carious teeth and bad breath.

And after he bathed and shaved, he was going to see Caitlin and say good-bye.

22

THE FIVE MEN WERE WAITING FOR JOHNNY AT THE Huerfano River where it flowed into the Arkansas. He should have seen them, should have known they were there, but he didn't, and they jumped him when he was crossing the river.

He had been following their tracks for three days, but the tracks were over two weeks old when he came upon them. He'd seen the hoofprints of Cutter's horse, and had realized he'd found the trail of the Maggards and Mike Purdy as well. He just hadn't expected to meet up with them this soon.

In that first instant, he saw Cutter and knew that they had been waiting for him to come along. They came out of concealment, and had evidently been waiting all this time, figuring he would be along eventually. He knew, too, that he had made a terrible mistake. He was not prepared for a gunfight. His rifle was still in its scabbard, and his pistols were out of reach except for the one he wore on his hip. But there wasn't even time to draw that. He saw the Maggards right behind Cutter, and with them the largest man he had ever seen, Mike Purdy.

They came riding into the water, guns blazing, and

Johnny felt the bullets tear into his face, into his torso, and he went off his horse and into the river. He disappeared under the waters in a swirl of blood, and was washed into the Arkansas, hurtling downstream, gasping for breath, trying to stay afloat.

"Come on, boys," said Cutter, "he's done for. Let's get on to Taos."

Johnny barely caught a glimpse of them as he was washed out of sight. A moment later, he came close to drowning in the strong current. He managed to push his head up above the swirling waters and gulp in a lungful of air before he went under again. He tumbled over and over, frantically trying to get his bearings in the swift-moving river, and the next thing he knew, he was slammed into a tree trunk at a bend, stopping his progress but very nearly pinning him underwater. He kicked and spluttered and found a branch for purchase. He pulled himself out of the current slowly and hung over the tree like a sack of meal, panting for breath, lights dancing in his head, and death so very close he could feel its hot breath on the back of his neck.

Johnny didn't know how long he hung there on that tree branch, but he finally was able to pull himself up and slowly crawl along the branch to reach the shore. He fell down on his face, exhausted, all of his energy drained away like the water and blood that dripped from his soaked buckskins.

Johnny should have died. He wanted to die. He had a bullet hole in his cheek and two more in his body. The balls had gone clean through, but he was in a bad way. He came to shore well downstream, where the Arkansas takes a bend, and he lay in the mud for half a day, packing his wounds, letting his body take the rest it needed.

Hunger tore at him, and the pain was almost unbearable. He thought of Caitlin and that supper she had invited him to, which he had had to turn down because of her father's dislike of him. It had been hard to say good-bye to her, but he knew that if he stayed, he would only bring her grief, and he didn't want that. She had begged him to stay, but he had sensed that if he did, he would not only be her prisoner, but her father's as well. So he had said farewell and ridden off, up the Arkansas, with fresh provisions in his saddlebags, new clothes, and an empty heart.

He crawled out of the mud and stifled the scream in his throat. He wanted to take the pistol and put it to his temple. But some inner spark flickered, and he dipped down deep inside himself and knew that he wanted to live. The hatred grew alongside the pain, and both of them overwhelmed him as he struggled to live. The river became his home, his sanctuary, and gave him food. He used the cold mud to heal the wound in his cheek and the holes in his body. He made snares and caught rabbits. He found pieces of flint and made curved fishhooks out of them, baited them with rabbit meat. He fought a rattlesnake over a field mouse and took the food from the snake's mouth, and ate both the mouse and snake.

In the long weeks that he healed, Johnny became stronger of will. He found an inner peace that he had never known, but always, underneath the placid coolness of his thoughts, were the smoldering fires of hatred.

He learned some things about himself and about survival as well. He saw the Utes coming, their faces painted for war, and he became part of the earth and did not move, did not blink an eye. He heard their talk and saw their faces, but he was stone and earth and he learned how to be invisible and breathe slow and shallow, how to hold in his scent. He saw Arapaho as well, and they passed him by without finding his tracks or seeing him.

All along his trail he'd thought of his father and the things his father had told him, had shown him. His father seemed to be part of him now, very real, very strong in his mind and in his daily life. Sometimes he wept, thinking about him. Sometimes he felt very tall and strong. His father's memory was something that sustained him, kept him going, made him see clearly.

Johnny began to observe the natural things, and he learned to hunt at night and find his way. He learned patience and stalking, and he learned how to find the center point of himself where there was clear thought and strength. It was as if he could go inside himself and find every answer he needed. Johnny began to realize that when he had nothing, he had everything. He saw that he could overcome any adversity by relying on himself and the natural things around him. If one wanted to be unseen, one became part of nature. If one wanted food, and that was the prime drive in all natural creatures that he observed, one found food or ways to obtain food. His nightmare was a great lesson, and it would stand him in good stead in the days to come.

He found his horse, but it was in bad shape. The animal had lost all strength in its legs, and its hide stretched over the bones so that Johnny could see its skeleton. He could not ride it without hurting deep inside, and finally had to destroy it. When he was strong, he set out on foot, following the Arkansas. He wore out his boots and made moccasins out of the tops. His clothes were ragged from wear and from using parts of them for fishing line. He grew lean and hard, and when he came to the first Mexican settlement, he looked like a man who had seen hell, and people looked into his eyes and turned away.

But the five men had passed through that place, and Johnny learned that they had gone to Taos.

With only his rifle and pistol, Johnny worked as a hunter for the settlers. When he had enough money he bought a horse and rode to the Fountain. There, he met McTeague, who was trapping in the area.

"I saw Cutter and the Maggards, that big fellow, Purdy," said McTeague.

"Where?" Johnny asked.

"In Taos. I expect they'll come back this way before the snow flies. Trappin' season's just about to start, when the beaver coats are prime."

"Why are you looking at me so funny?"

"I thought you were dead, Johnny."

"I was."

"You talk peculiar."

"I am peculiar," Johnny said with a cock-eyed grin breaking over his teeth.

"Why don't you stay up and trap with me this winter. You'll put some gold in your pocket."

"I'm not giving up on Cutter," Johnny replied.

"They'll kill you for sure next time," McTeague told him. "Those are hard men."

"How can they kill a man they already believe to be dead?" Some of the bitterness came through in his tone.

"Still wantin' vengeance, eh?"

"It's not vengeance I want, Cal. It's justice I'm after."

But he knew there was a price to pay—for everything. What price, he wondered, must he forfeit to balance the blind woman's scales of justice? And where did the law begin? Where did it end? He thought of his father and his father's dreams and the way he died, without dignity, penniless, unable to fill out the rest of his life as a man of property and accomplishment. Yes, Johnny knew, the bitterness went deep, and the questions nagged at him like blowflies at a raw wound. He had decided that his father's death would mean nothing unless those who conspired to murder him also realized how precious breath is, how much life is worth. "I was the learner before," he told himself. "Now maybe I better do some teaching." About life. About death.

23

JOHNNY HAD READ THE FEW REMAINING PAGES HE HAD managed to save of *The Odyssey* twice in those days of healing and wandering, and he saw himself tracing an ancient path, feeling he had somehow incurred the wrath of the same gods who had tortured Ulysses, who had thrown obstacles in his path, who had kept him away from his home in Ithaca.

Perhaps, he thought, he should have stayed with McTeague and trapped for the winter. He still had some money, but he had little else. He had not found Cutter, who seemed as elusive as shadows on water.

He kept crossing Cutter's trail, and hearing of him and the Maggards and that man Mike Purdy, who was, many said, as big as a bear and twice as mean. One thing he knew. Cutter and the Maggard brothers had not gone back to trap the Fountain. And Johnny wondered if Cutter had gone back to civilization, to Sibley perhaps, or even to St. Louis. But somehow, he knew Cutter was still in the mountains or nearby. The Rockies were a hiding place for a great many men like Cutter. And now he knew that any man who stayed in the high places became as wild as any

Indian, as wild as any creature that dwelled high above the plains.

And the old Johnny was dead, he knew, and he was now as wild as the deer that roamed the high meadows. Something inside him had changed. He had gone into the mountains, but now, he knew, the mountains had come into him as well.

He began to avoid all travelers after seeing McTeague, but he knew that men would see him in the distance, and he knew they wondered about him. He could see them stop and point and talk and then ride on, shaking their heads.

When he returned to Taos after seeing McTeague up on the Fountain, he slipped in during the night. He had let his beard grow and when he visited the cantinas in search of word about Cutter, he was quiet, unobtrusive. He listened, asked no questions.

He heard a few times about the men he was looking for, and in this way he began to learn their habits, their peculiarities when they were back in civilization.

It was after that long winter that Johnny began to hunt them again, for he had gotten word that they had returned to the pueblos of Taos and Santa Fe and that they believed that he was dead and no longer a danger to them.

But Johnny had a plan.

He became a Mexican. He wore a serape, sandals, and a sombrero. He spoke little, and even bought the white trousers and shirt the peons wore. He smoked the thin brown cigars and drank the tequila. He never spoke his name, and people wondered about him, wondered who he was. He was thought to be addled, or even crazed, by some.

One bold Mexican asked him one day point-blank in Spanish *"Quien eres?"* "Who are you?"

Johnny had answered, also in Spanish. *"Quizás soy Telemachus."* "Maybe I'm Telemachus."

The Mexican fled in terror because he did not understand what Johnny was saying.

So Johnny became a kind of legend, an ominous figure in Taos. His legend became unnerving to the Cutter bunch, who were wary of every stranger as a natural part of their existence.

The Mexicans called Johnny The Silent One at first. Then, as their curiosity grew stronger, they asked him where he was going, why he was in Taos.

"I ride to the sunset," Johnny said.

And that is all that he said. So the townspeople began to speak of him as The Sunset Rider, and that was poetic enough to suit them. The term appealed to their dark minds, their sense of mystery.

One day, Johnny was sitting at a table in a dark corner of a cantina when the *mozo* who was wiping the tables stopped to talk in whispers.

"It is the big one you are looking for, I think. Is this not so?"

"I am looking for the one called El Cortador. I look for him, and him only."

"Ah, The Cutter, yes. I have seen him with the big one and the three brothers."

"When did you see them?" Johnny asked, suddenly interested.

"I saw them at the house of Clarita last night. They were very drunk. They asked if the tall gringo was still looking for them. The one they call Juanito. Johnny."

"And what were they told?"

"They were told many things. They were very frightened, I think. The one you call The Cutter, he drink too much and they carry him away. The three brothers go with The Cutter, and the big one, El Oso, The Bear, he stays with the girls. He is too big to move. Maybe he is still there."

"At Clarita's," Johnny said.

"That might be," the man said.

Stagg went to Clarita's and found Mike Purdy there. Mike was sitting with a pair of painted whores when Johnny entered. The girls seemed to recognize Johnny and they got up from the table, leaving Purdy alone.

Johnny walked over to the table and looked at Purdy with a cold stare.

"Who are you, stranger?" Purdy asked, his tongue loosened by strong drink.

"The name's Johnny Stagg."

"Haw! Stagg's wolf meat. At the bottom of the Arkansas or bones on the bank."

"Look close, Purdy," he said, "real close, and then tell Cutter and the Maggards I'm still on their track."

"I don't know who the hell you are, mister, but I ain't no messenger."

Purdy clawed for the pistol stuck in his waistband, a .60-caliber Spanish weapon that was huge. But in Purdy's hand, the pistol looked no bigger than a derringer.

"I figured you'd do this," Johnny said, snatching his pistol cleanly from its holster. Before Purdy could cock the hammer on his pistol, Johnny aimed and fired. Purdy cried out in pain as the ball smashed into his arm. His fingers opened and his pistol fell from his grasp, clattered to the floor. The whores sped away from Purdy like a pair of prairie hens flushed from cover, their colorful skirts swishing and flashing like the chips in a kaleidoscope. Both women screamed in terror as a cloud of white smoke hung in the air.

Johnny stepped in close and kicked Purdy's gun across the floor. It spun like a top, and stopped when it clanged into a brass spittoon at the bar. Johnny peeled back a section of his own hard-bristle, thick beard. There was a streak of dark flesh creasing the pink of Johnny's cheek. He opened his shirt and there were lumps of similarly ravaged flesh, like angry ropes, crisscrossing his torso as if they were maps of pain and torture, scrawled drawings of badlands etched into a man's flesh like horrible, diabolical tattoos.

Purdy's eyes widened. He swallowed hard.

"Next time I see you, I'll kill you," Stagg said, and he turned on his heel and walked away from the shaken and bleeding man. He walked out the door and into the night as Purdy whimpered in pain and clutched his arm in an attempt to stop the flow of blood.

24

JOHNNY SAT IN THE SHADE ON A BENCH IN THE PLAZA of the pueblo of Taos, his sombrero brim slanted to hide his bearded face, his pistol concealed inside his white trousers and overlapping white shirt. He was smoking a cigarillo to complete his disguise as a Mexican peon.

That was when he saw her, on the other side of the plaza, emerging from a carriage with her father. His senses left him for a moment and he thought he might be mistaken, but no, it was Caitlin and she wore a pretty sun-yellow dress and had a blue ribbon tied in her hair. Her father went into an office and she stayed outside, talking to a little boy and his sister who were walking by with their mother.

She spoke perfect Spanish, which surprised him at first, until he realized how much time had passed since he had seen her. She was even prettier now than she was when he first met her, and he did not see any rings on her fingers.

For a moment, he was tempted to walk across the plaza and speak to her. He put out the cigarillo, and was about to stand up when her father emerged from the building, accompanied by another man.

The other man appeared disheveled and unkempt, and he blinked his eyes and shaded them with his hand. When he turned away from the sun, Johnny saw his face clearly. The man with Seamus O'Brien was none other than Cletus Maggard. As the two men stood there, a soldier came out of the building carrying a pistol, a possibles pouch, and two powder horns. He gave these to O'Brien, who then handed them to Maggard. The soldier disappeared back inside the building after saluting O'Brien.

The muscles in Johnny's jaw tightened as he saw Maggard nod to Caitlin while he slung on his possibles pouch and powder horns. He thrust his pistol inside his belt.

Johnny had heard that Cutter and the Maggards were back in Taos, and that was why he was there. He knew that one or all of them sooner or later would come to the large, tree-dotted plaza, but he'd never expected to see the eldest Maggard with Caitlin and her father.

Johnny saw O'Brien point in a direction that Maggard followed with his gaze. Maggard nodded. The two men shook hands. Caitlin got back in the carriage with her father, and Maggard walked in the direction O'Brien had pointed, and Johnny figured that was where Maggard's horse was stabled. His own horse was tied in the shade nearby.

The carriage pulled away as Johnny got to his feet. He started walking across the plaza. Caitlin looked out, and he could swear she was staring straight at him. Her gaze lingered for a long moment, and then the carriage was gone. He wondered if she knew who the tall Mexican really was, and he half hoped the carriage would turn around and she would jump out and run up to him, put her arms around him.

Johnny followed Maggard to the small livery stable, but did not go inside. He leaned against the adobe wall near a window to see if he could hear what Maggard might be up to.

"Ho, Clete. I see you got out."

"Yep, Seamus paid the duty and some bribes. We can deliver the goods tonight."

Johnny's heartbeat quickened when he heard the other man's voice. It sounded familiar, but at first he couldn't place whose it was. It didn't sound like Nate's, so he didn't think it was Jedediah. But he was sure it belonged to someone he knew.

"My horse ready?" he heard Cletus Maggard say.

"He's saddled up."

"Well, come on then. Cutter will be waiting for us."

"Cutter said Mike would meet us and take us to the warehouse. When will O'Brien pick up the wagons?"

"In a couple of hours," Cletus said. "He's got drovers coming for them."

"I hope he'll have our money for us."

"Frank, you worry too damned much. Seamus always pays."

"I know. He always paid us when I rode with Marsh and them."

"It's that damned Mike I'm worried about," Cletus said. "Ever since he got shot by Stagg, he's actin' spooky. And he's got broken bones in his arm that are causin' him a heap of pain. He's married to that mescal."

"I know. I don't trust Purdy," Early said. "He could make trouble for us."

"I'm going to tell Cutter to get rid of him before we set out again."

"You mean kill him, Clete?"

"No, I mean send him packin'. Frank, you got my knife I left with you?"

"Here, Clete. I knew O'Brien would bail you out and pay them Mexes off."

"Well, he did, and they had some good drinkin' whiskey in that *juzgado*. And the pretty women come in last night."

"I thought they'd throw away the key on you."

Maggard laughed. "Them Mexes all had their hands out. They won't bother us no more."

Johnny stiffened. Now he knew who the other man was. Frank Early, one of the trappers he had ridden with. So, he had thrown in with the Maggards and Cutter. Johnny wasn't surprised about that. He was surprised that Caitlin's father would have anything to do with Cutter. He wondered if Caitlin knew who her father was dealing with.

The two men spoke some more, but Johnny had already heard enough. He walked away from the stable and went to his horse, a finely bred Spanish horse that was part Arabian, part Andalusian. He had bought it in Santa Fe from a Mexican who drove horses up from the Rio Bravo. Luckily, Johnny had kept his money in his saddlebags, which he was able to find after being ambushed by Cutter and his bunch. He had never found his father's rifle or the other two pistols, however. He had only his .40-caliber, which he no longer carried in a holster, but under his sash, concealed behind the waistband. Except for his height, he looked like any Mexican with his deep tan and heavy beard.

The horse was a gelding, around fifteen hands high, coal black, with small feet, good lungs, a small star blaze on its forehead. He called it Sunset.

A few minutes later, he followed Cletus and Frank as they rode to a street where there were several cantinas. They stopped at one of them, El Tecolate, and while Maggard waited outside, Early went inside. He emerged a few moments later with Mike Purdy, who appeared to be slightly drunk. The big man had his arm in a sling, and was holding onto it as if he was in pain.

Purdy untied a horse at the hitch rail and climbed awkwardly into the saddle. The three men rode off through the narrow dusty streets of the town. They came to an adobe warehouse near the road to Santa Fe, south of the pueblo of Taos.

Johnny held back and did not follow where he might be seen.

Johnny tied Sunset to a small juniper in a grove of trees, and found a place not far away where he could watch the warehouse and not be seen. He took up a position behind a growth of scrub pines and scraggly brush.

Johnny saw a place where he could sneak up to the warehouse around the back. There was a small wash that cut through the brush and crossed the road. He ducked down and followed it until he came to the back, where he saw horses tied. He recognized Cutter's horse and a couple of others that belonged to the Maggard brothers.

He slipped up to the warehouse without being seen, and hunkered down next to a window. He heard loud voices coming from inside. He recognized Purdy's whining deep voice right away.

"I'm clearing out, Cutter. Maybe you better do the same. It's you he's after, you know. I told you he said to tell you that."

"You're runnin' scared, Mike," Cutter said.

"Damned right I am. That bastard Stagg is pure devil with a gun. 'Sides, I got to see a sawbones and see if he can't fix this blamed arm."

"Have him look at your bull head, too, Mike," Cletus said.

Johnny heard them all laugh at that.

"I still want my cut from this silver we got here," Purdy said.

"You'll get paid. O'Brien won't be here for another hour or so. I'll bring you your money." Cletus Maggard was the one who spoke, Johnny knew.

"I'll take it from you, Cutter. I don't like any of you damned Maggards."

"The feelin's mutual," Jedediah said. He sounded a lot like his twin, Nate, Johnny thought.

"In fact, we never did like you much, Mike," young Elijah said. "You're fat as a pig and stink like a skunk."

"You ain't no flower yourself, Lijah," Purdy said.

"All right," Cutter said. "You got money comin', Mike. Where do you want me to meet you? We won't be here by the time you finish with the doc."

"I'll be at Rosa's, up in the north of the pueblo."

"Why there?"

"Because it ain't lit up and Stagg probably don't know about it."

"You think he's follerin' you around, Mike?" This from Cletus.

"I ain't takin' no chances."

"Well, I'm going by that way anyway," Cutter said. "You know that hideout where I been stayin'?"

"Yeah, up in the mountains."

"The Maggards are going to Santa Fe with O'Brien, in case of bandits. I'm going to hole up until they get back."

"We'll ride ten miles with O'Brien," Cletus told Cutter, "then meet you at the hideout late tonight."

"Can't I stay with you, Cutter?" Purdy asked.

"I want you as far away from me as you can get, Mike. If Stagg's a-follerin' you, I sure as hell don't want you bringin' him to me."

More laughter.

"Shit," Purdy said.

"Go on, Mike," Cutter told Purdy.

"Don't you forget now, Cutter. I'll be needin' that *dinero*."

"See you in a hour or so."

Johnny had heard enough. He was glad Purdy's horse was still tied out front with Early's and Cletus's mounts. But he knew he had to leave now or risk being seen when the others came out back to get their horses.

By the time he reached Sunset, Purdy was riding toward town.

Johnny mounted up and prepared to follow Purdy at a distance.

But he wasn't worried about losing sight of Purdy. He knew where Rosa's cantina was, and if Cutter went there later, he'd sure as hell have a message waiting for him.

25

AFTER PURDY LEFT THE DOCTOR'S ADOBE OFFICE, HE seemed to know that someone was following him. He kept looking back over his shoulder, but Johnny made sure that all he saw was a Mexican slumped over on a horse, seemingly in a drunken stupor. A common sight in Taos, Johnny knew. He also knew that Purdy didn't know Sunset was his horse.

Johnny saw Purdy when the big man entered the saloon. He waited outside, watching for Cutter until late in the evening. He sensed that Cutter was not going to come and pay Purdy off.

Finally, as Johnny waited in the shadows across the street from Rosa's, he saw Purdy stagger out and laboriously climb onto his horse. Purdy headed north on the road bordering El Rio Grande del Norte. The moon was up and the skies clear, so he had no difficulty following Purdy at a distance.

Finally Purdy left the road and headed east into broken country. It was after midnight when Johnny saw the adobe, atop a hill. There were two horses in a corral out back, and the light from a lamp was glowing through the front windows. He watched as Purdy rode up, dismounted, and walked up to the door. Johnny circled the cabin and found a place to ground-tie Sunset. He looked at the horses in the corral and saw that one of them at least, perhaps both, belonged to Cutter.

He walked back out to a place where he could see Purdy. Apparently the front door was latched, because Purdy was still standing there. Then Johnny heard a pounding noise and saw Purdy banging on the door.

"Cutter, damn you, open the door."

"Go away, Mike," Cutter yelled through the door at Purdy.

"I want my money," Purdy said.

The door opened and Johnny saw Cutter standing there, holding a small cloth sack. He thrust it at Purdy.

"Here's your damned money, Mike. Now get the hell out and don't come back. I don't want Stagg comin' out here."

"Can't I come in? I think Stagg's been follerin' me."

Cutter stepped up to the open doorway. "No, Mike," he said. "Go on back to town."

"He's goin' to kill me, Cutter."

"Who?"

"Stagg. He said so."

"Go on then. He's your problem, not mine."

The door slammed, and Purdy stood there for a moment or two. Then he tucked the sack in his waistband and lurched back to his horse, cursing under his breath. Johnny walked back to his horse and climbed into the saddle. He heard Purdy riding away, and as Johnny rode past the adobe, he saw that the lamps had been doused.

Johnny rode a wide loop so that he could get ahead of Purdy. He waited along the trail, not far from the adobe hideout. Purdy was hardly moving, but he was coming. Johnny wondered if he had fallen asleep in the saddle.

Johnny waited, a shadowy figure atop his horse, ghostly in the twilight.

Purdy rode up on him. Johnny pulled his pistol out of his waistband. He watched as Purdy's head jerked up in recognition. Purdy pulled on his reins and came to a full stop yards away from Johnny.

"That you, Stagg?"

"It's me. I've got a pistol aimed at your gut, Purdy."

"You said—hell, you ain't killin' me."

"No," Johnny said. "We're going back to that adobe and you're going to tell Cutter I'm here."

"You bastard," snarled Purdy. "Go tell him yourself. He'll probably shoot me if I show my face up there again. You've got all of us real spooked, Stagg."

"I'll shoot you if you don't turn your horse around and ride back up there."

"Look, you want money, Stagg? I've got money here." Purdy pulled the sack of money out of his waistband, held it up for Johnny to see.

"I don't want you or your money. I came here for Cutter."

"He'll kill us both," Purdy said.

"I'll take that chance."

Johnny rode up and thrust his pistol in Purdy's face. Then he reached over and lifted Purdy's pistol from his waistband. He stuck it under his own belt. Then he knocked the sack of money out of Purdy's hand.

"You can pick that up later, Purdy. Now turn your horse around and get moving, or I'll drop you right here and now."

"You sonofabitch," Purdy muttered.

But he turned his horse around and started riding back to Cutter's adobe. Johnny stayed right behind him so that from the front, it looked as if a single rider was coming up to the adobe. At least he hoped that was so.

When they were close enough, Johnny ordered Purdy to dismount. Johnny stepped out of his saddle and ground-tied Sunset to a clump of greasewood.

"Walk up to the door," Johnny said. "I'll be right behind you."

When Purdy got to the door, Johnny stepped to one side, his pistol trained on his prisoner. "Knock hard," he whispered. Purdy banged on the door with both fists.

"Who's there?" Cutter called out.

Purdy looked at Johnny. Johnny nodded.

"It's me, Mike," Purdy said loudly, his tongue thick with drink.

"What in hell do you want now?"

Johnny nodded to Purdy again. "Tell him you've got something for him," he whispered.

"I've got something for you, Cutter."

The door opened suddenly and Cutter lunged forward, the Arkansas toothpick in his hand. "I've got something for you, Mike," Cutter said, shoving the knife into Purdy's abdomen. Purdy grunted and staggered backward, blood spurting from his belly.

A pale yellow light flowed from the open doorway as Cutter withdrew his knife, then leaped forward, slashing at Purdy's throat. The knife cut half of Purdy's neck in two, and blood burst from the wound like a crimson fountain. Purdy dropped to his knees.

Johnny made a sound as he leaped toward Cutter's back. He grabbed Cutter's arm with his left hand. Purdy spun around and knocked the pistol out of Johnny's hand, but Johnny held onto the arm holding the knife.

The two men grappled as Purdy collapsed, mortally wounded, unable to speak because of the wound that had severed his vocal chords and part of his spine.

Cutter and Johnny staggered backward and went through the doorway of the adobe. Cutter tried to jerk his arm away from Johnny's grip, but Johnny pushed hard and tightened his fingers around Cutter's forearm.

"Damn you, Stagg," Cutter breathed.

Johnny looked Cutter in the eye and kneed him in the

groin. Cutter crumpled, and Johnny slid his hand down and wrested the knife from Cutter's hand. Cutter lunged for it with his other hand. Johnny slashed at him, and the knife caught Cutter's thumb edgewise.

The surgically sharp blade sliced through the thumb and took away two of Cutter's fingers. Cutter screamed in pain, and Johnny forced him down to the floor. The knife blade continued its course as the two men fell, Johnny landing on top of Cutter's back.

Cutter's hand hit the floor and Johnny's weight forced the knife blade downward, cutting off the remaining fingers of Cutter's hand. Cutter snarled in rage and turned over. He lashed out at Johnny with his good hand.

Johnny stabbed at it with the knife and the point went through Cutter's palm. Blood spurted from the wound, splashing Johnny's hand and wrist.

Cutter closed his hand around the knife blade and tried to knock it out of his palm. Johnny twisted the slender knife blade and pulled it on a slant away from the palm. The blade carved out a chunk of palm and ripped through bone and sinew, cutting off Cutter's middle and index fingers and his thumb.

Johnny kicked out and his boot caught Cutter in the chest, knocking him flat on his back. Cutter screamed as blood streamed from his mutilated hands. He held them up and screamed again. As he lay there, Johnny got to his feet and stared down at Cutter, panting for breath.

Tears streamed down Cutter's face. He let his hands fall to the floor and began sobbing.

Then Cutter looked up at Johnny, his face grimacing in pain.

"You murdered my father, Cutter," Johnny said.

"Yeah, you sonofabitch. I stabbed him. Cut him. Kill me. Jesus, Stagg, end it. End it now."

"No. I'm just going to leave you here, Cutter. I am all out of vengeance. I never wanted killing. Never wanted to kill a man or see a man die. Not in pain, like my pa. I have had enough of killing. Some say vengeance is the Lord's, and I go along with that. You do what you can do here. You can live if you've a mind to and a gut to stomach the hard of it. I'm just going and leaving what's left of life to you. I want you to think about that moment when you plunged your knife into my father's back. Just think about it while you decide whether to live or die here in this adobe."

"You cut my hands off."

Johnny looked at the bloodstained knife in his hands. Then he threw it to the dirt floor. The blade stuck in the ground and the knife quivered for several seconds.

"You won't be stabbing anybody again, Cutter," Johnny said. "Unless you can manage to cut your own throat."

Johnny started for the door. But something caught his eye and he walked over to a corner where there was a trunk. Next to it, leaning against the wall, was his father's rifle. He picked it up, opened the trunk. Inside were his father's pistol and Nate Maggard's, the one Nate had used to pistol-whip Bill Stagg.

Johnny lifted the pistols in their holsters and walked toward the door, carrying the Lancaster rifle. He stopped and looked at Cutter.

"My guess," he said to Cutter, "is that you won't know how to die, because you didn't know how to live."

He walked outside and closed the door. He picked up his own pistol and tucked it into his waistband. Moments later, he was on Sunset.

As he rode away, he heard Cutter screaming and cursing. Johnny drew in a deep breath of the night air and looked up at the stars.

He felt close to his father just then, as close as if he were still alive.

It was a good feeling.

26

JOHNNY STARED AT THE FOUR MEN'S FACES. HE COULD
hardly believe his eyes. He'd never expected to see anything like that in Santa Fe.

But there they were, the three Maggard brothers and
Frank Early, hanging from the gallows, their bodies twisting slowly in the slight breeze that blew across the plaza.

The crowd began to break up, drift away, some of them
speaking in whispered tones to each other in the soft liquid sibilants of the Spanish tongue.

"Cabrónes."

"Hijos de mala leche."

"Ladrónes."

As the crowd dispersed, Johnny saw a carriage off to
the side of the plaza. There were a number of soldiers
nearby, talking among themselves. There were some officials standing in the shade, but he couldn't see their
faces.

"De vez en cuando, hay justicia en el mundo," a man
said as he walked away.

How true, Johnny thought. Sometimes there is justice
in this world.

He stopped another man and spoke to him in Spanish.

"What happened here?" he asked. "Why were those men hanged?"

Before the man could answer, Johnny felt a tug on his sleeve. He turned around, slightly irritated, and then his mouth dropped open.

"Because they tried to rob my father while they were escorting us to Santa Fe," Caitlin said. "They were caught, tried, found guilty, and hanged."

"Caitlin."

"I thought that was you in the plaza in Taos. Why didn't you say hello?"

"I—I had some things to do," he said.

"I almost didn't recognize you in that beard. But in my heart, I knew it was you, Johnny."

"You look beautiful, Caitlin. I've missed you."

He could smell the delicate aroma of her perfume. She smelled of lilacs and honeysuckle and morning glories.

"Did you finish what you had to do?" she asked, moving closer to him.

"Yes."

"Cutter?" she asked.

Johnny nodded.

"Did you—did you . . . ?"

"I didn't kill him, if that's what you're asking. But he'll never use a knife again. On anyone."

"Good, I'm glad. Will you be going back home now? Back to Sibley?"

"I don't know," Johnny said. "Are you going back to St. Louis?"

Caitlin shook her head, but she was smiling. As if she was happy.

"Will you stay here?" he asked.

"My father has been talking about a new land. Beyond the mountains. A place called California. They say it's always warm there and people will travel twenty miles just to see a person shake with the ague."

Johnny laughed. Caitlin laughed, too.

"I've never heard of it," he said.

"It's supposed to be a paradise," she said.

"Do you want to go there?"

"I might, if a certain person were to go there."

"Who?" he asked, a tremor in his voice, a fluttering in his stomach, a slight quiver in his knees.

"A man I could love and trust. Someone strong and faithful and loving to me."

"Do you know anyone like that?" he asked.

"I might," she said with a coy smile.

"Is California to the west, where the sun sets?"

"It's as far west as you can go," she said. "It stops at the sea, the beautiful sea."

"It sounds like a place I might like to go to."

She put her arm in his.

"Come with me," she said. "Let's talk to my father, and I want you to meet my mother. You'll like her."

"I like her daughter," he said.

"Her daughter likes you, too, Johnny."

Johnny hesitated. "But your father doesn't like me."

Caitlin smiled. "Oh, I think he's changed his mind about you, especially since he had the trouble with the Maggard boys and Frank."

"I hope so," Johnny said.

Then she squeezed his arm, and he felt light-headed. As they walked across the plaza toward the carriage, he saw her father in the shade saying good-bye to the officials. Her mother waved at them.

"California," he said. "Sounds nice."

"They say the sunsets on the ocean are beautiful."

"Yes, I'll bet they are."

And he squeezed her arm and floated along beside her, not thinking about Sibley or what had happened to his father and him, and he was glad that Caitlin had recognized him. He knew he was more fortunate than Ulysses had been when he returned to Ithaca, old, bearded, forgotten, no one, not even his son, Telemachus, recognizing him. Only his dog.

California, he thought. It had a melodious flow to it, that word, like music, like a song a man might sing to his sweetheart while he watched the sun setting golden in the west, spreading honey over the sea, welcoming a man home, welcoming the wanderer back to his home by the honey-golden sea.

ON 522-8

The 5/16/02 an Ben
Stillman. Then the past came looking for an on the
Hi-line, ranchers are being rustled out of their livelihoods...and
their lives. The son of an old friend suspects that these rustlers
have murdered his fa is too crooked to get any
straight answers, but old marshal live up to the
legend the bandown to administer

BLOOD MOUNTAIN 0-425-16976-6

Stra at the a train of settlers is by a outlaws ram-
pa hrough he mountains the
wrong man, nothing on Earth to stop paying every
one of them in blood.

DATE DUE

AUG 1 9 2002		MAY 0 7 2011	
JAN 0 2 2004		JUL 2 7 2011	
APR 2 2 2004		AUG 1 0 2011	
JUN 0 5 2004		NOV 1 2 2011	
10/18 P			
DEC 2 7 2006			
MAY 0 3 2007			
JUL 1 2 2007			
MAY 1 1 2009			
JUL 1 4 2009			
JAN 1 6 2010			
JAN 0 6 2011			
GAYLORD			PRINTED IN U.S.A.

"Make oom on yo r out of favorites

Pe er Brand old will be g out a claim the re."
Roderus

TO ORDER CALL
00-6262